Boy · Youth · Man

A Triptych of Novellas

Joseph Maiolo

Overcoat Books
Duluth, Minnesota

Overcoat Books
An imprint of X-Communication
118 Chester Parkway
Duluth, Minnesota 55805
218-310-6541

Boy • youth • man: a triptych of novellas

Copyright © 2012 by Joseph Maiolo.

All rights reserved. No part of this book may be reproduced or transmitted in any form by any means without written permission from the publisher.

Cover painting "Portrait of a Concerned Stranger" by Julie Maiolo

Cover and interior design and layout by Tony Dierckins

An earlier version of "A Boy's Tale" was previously published under the title *Elverno*.

An earler version of "Man of Letters" was previously published in *The Texas Review*, Fall/Winter 1985 (Vol. VI, No.s 3 & 4).

First Edition, 2012

12 13 14 15 16 • 5 4 3 2 1

Library of Congress Control Number: 2012901912

ISBN: 978-1-887317-91-7

Printed in the U.S.A.

A Boy's Tale *is for my big brother, Michael,*
who ran touchdowns and led interference for me

The Error of the Rings *is for my little sister, Angela,*
who watched and waited and couldn't wait

Man of Letters *is in memory of*
Peter Taylor, George Garrett, Richard Yates, and James Dickey
and for Fred Chappell

— J.M.

~

Also by Joseph Maiolo and Overcoat Books:

My Turkish Missile Crisis (a memoir)

Contents

A Boy's Tale 1

The Error of the Rings 65

Man of Letters 101

A Boy's Tale

A Boy's Tale

"...only a...boy...peeling a twig, a child beside a weenywhite steed."
— James Joyce, Finnegans Wake

We hadn't seen or heard from our father in over six months. My brother and I had been living with our grandmother while Mother worked in Richmond. But the town priest told Grandmother and Mother (when she was visiting us) that since Vince and I were starting to run around and get into trouble we should go to a nice school for boys. And he had found just the one. So they made the arrangements, and we found ourselves, with Mother, on a bus heading for Cincinnati.

It was night. When Mother had told us that we were going to a school, just for a year, where we would stay "night and day" and where we would be taken care of properly and given what we needed, I felt kind of sorry for her because of the way she said it. But there were those words again—"what we needed"—and so I began to think that maybe they were trying to make up for our troubles by sending us off to school. "Remember that you're brothers and look out for each other," she told us, but mainly Vince. She'd always said that when we moved.

Uncle Pasco was waiting for us at the bus station. Mother hugged him, and he introduced his friend Freddy, who would put us up in his apartment for the night. Uncle Pasco and Freddy both ruffled our hair and said things with "boys" in them. Then the men took our bags and we went to the car, dodging people with shopping bags and suitcases, and we drove off into the city.

Uncle Pasco gave Mother his place on the couch, and Vince and I slept on the floor on a pallet. When Uncle Pasco began to settle into a chair for the night, Freddy came out of the bedroom in his pajamas and said he could sleep with him.

Mother woke me during the night and told me to go to the bathroom, and as I stumbled along in front of her, my eyes full of sleep, I was not aware of where I was until she turned on the bathroom light. I told her that I really didn't have to go, but she said I'd better try anyway, that we were in somebody else's house now. So I did, and managed a small trickle. As I shivered at the end, which caused my head to turn, I saw that her face was averted and I heard a sniffle. I didn't want to make it any harder on her, so I turned back, lifted my shorts, and brushed past her as if I wanted to get back to bed in a hurry.

It was chilly, and after I slipped between the cotton blankets I snuggled up to Vince as close as I could without actually touching him. Mother had stayed behind in the bathroom, and at first I thought she just wanted to use it herself. Time passed, and as I thought about her in there I started to wake Vince. But it was cold and I was tired and the cover was warm. After a while she came and took her place on the couch, and I slept.

The next morning Uncle Pasco drove us to the school in Freddy's car. Vince and I rode in the back, looking out at the big buildings and the crowds of people. As we passed sprawling factories, their chimneys sending high columns of smoke to mix with the clouds, we laughed and played around, but when we came to the outskirts of the city, a sudden quiet settled into the car. It was as if I had just remembered that I'd left a boy behind, an old friend, and I wanted to stop the car and go back to get him. It seemed that the trees had left their roots and were whizzing by. I'd pressed my face against the car window to keep the tears from showing.

We had come to the open country of farmhouses and barns and animals, and I pulled back to find that the trees were still as they always were. Vince gave his wry smile, and it came to me that he might have felt the same way, long before. After a while, Uncle Pasco turned onto a treeless road that wound through the grounds of some holy, hushed place.

As we drove through the entrance with a sign chiseled in stone—Mount St. Francis, School for Boys, 1923—Mother turned to us with the smile she gave us at times like this. "It looks pretty nice. What do you think, boys?"

"It reminds me of an army camp I was stationed at," Uncle Pasco said.

"Quiet!" Mother said, in Italian.

But Uncle Pasco was always joking that way. Mother was just in a bad mood, even though she'd asked the question of Vince and me as pleasantly as she could. I was sufficiently recovered by then, after having kissed my Saint Christopher medal, and I was even a little impressed by the place, for across the way I saw some grazing horses which, as we moved on, disappeared beyond a rise.

Uncle Pasco parked the car, and we walked up the steps of the main building, carrying our bags. In the anteroom, the first thing I noticed was that hollow sound footsteps make in such places, then pictures of Jesus and Mary and some saints. I recognized Saint Anthony by his bald spot and because he was holding Jesus as a baby. We put our bags down, and in a minute a brother entered in a brown, hooded robe tied at the waist with a white rope with a rosary and a cross attached to it. He was a little shabby and bent-over, and he wore sandals.

"Yes?" he said.

"I have brought my sons," Mother said.

"Your name?"

"Mrs. Florentino."

"You may take seats in there." He guided us to a large waiting room. "I will see if the headmaster is expecting you." He walked out with his hands in opposite loose sleeves, like he was cold.

The room was not meant for waiting in very long, or else forever. Like a hospital, it seemed to require respect and silence for the sick and dying. But in a corner stood a statue, taller than I was, of Saint Francis in bare feet and robe. He had a bird in his hand and one on his shoulder, and I recalled the same likeness of him on a card I had been given at Bible school that summer. The back of the card had a prayer on it. I could see the words in my head—Canticle of the Sun—but I still couldn't say the strange one without it first coming out "can tickle." Even Sister Agnes had laughed, at first.

In a few minutes a man walked in briskly, smiling at Mother. He was big and strong, with rough hands. He looked like the football player on cereal boxes, but he was a brother like the other one, except his robe was clean and pressed and his rope and rosary and cross were neatly lined up. He shook back the wide sleeves of his robe and straightened the hood.

"Hello, Father," Mother said.

"Brother Lawrence," he said.

"But aren't you the one in charge?"

"The headmaster, yes. Brother Lawrence. And you are Mrs. Florentino, and these are—. I thought you had only two sons."

Uncle Pasco made his small manhood better known by getting up. But he wasn't mad, good thing.

"I'm sorry," the headmaster said. Then he lowered his voice, but we could all still hear him. "The boys' *father*?"

Vince should have looked at me and laughed, but he didn't.

Mother gave a pained smile. "My brother."

The headmaster nodded to Uncle Pasco, who started to put out his hand, but didn't. "And the boys, I see."

"That's Vincent." Mother touched my head. "Cosimo."

"Yes, boys. Now, Mrs. Florentino, would you come into my office where we can talk?" He escorted Mother out of the room. As soon as they were gone, Uncle Pasco began joking and ruffling our hair. His voice sounded like thunder in that echo chamber, and I was afraid that someone was going to come in and ask us to quiet down. Uncle Pasco gave Vince a two-dollar bill and told him to split it with me. "And some Sunday," he said, "me and Freddy will come out and take you to see the Reds play." By the time Mother and the headmaster came back, I was glad that Uncle Pasco had to calm down. I didn't feel like messing around anymore.

When the headmaster told us about the ponies and how we would be able to ride them during our recreation hours, I perked up, even though Mother was blowing her nose. The headmaster gave Uncle Pasco a signal, and Uncle Pasco tried to help Mother leave us. We got her to the room with the outside door.

"Mrs. Florentino, pull yourself together. Uh, *you*!" he said to Vince. "Say something to her." He began pacing around.

"When can we ride the ponies?"

I saw what Vince was doing. "Yeah, when?" I said, so cheerfully I almost made myself feel all right.

"As soon as they leave, I'll give you a tour of the place." Brother Lawrence tried to speak above Mother's crying. "Then maybe you can see the ponies." He saw that it wasn't working, and walked disgustedly to the other room.

"Hurry up, Mother, and go," Vince said.

The three of us got her to the door, but she grabbed the doorjamb and held on. "It's not fair!" she screamed. "How about him!"

I knew who she meant.

Finally we got her out the door. Only I had to hug her two more times.

❧ ❧ ❧

Brother Lawrence called for the shabby brother to help Vince and me carry our bags, and Brother Lawrence led the way to the dormitory. It was one large room: beds in rows, lockers around all the walls. We stood in the doorway, as Brother Lawrence told the shabby one to set the bags down and return to the administration building. Another brother came out of a little room nearby.

"These are the two new boys," Brother Lawrence said. "This is Brother Felix. He is in charge of the dormitory, day and night. And he works in the dispensary on Tuesday and Thursday."

"What's that?" I said.

"It's where you go if you get sick," Brother Felix said, kindly. "And what would you like me to call you?" We told him, and he said, "Welcome to Mount Saint Francis, Vince, Casey."

"Give them their bed assignments and a locker, Brother," said Brother Lawrence. He seemed impatient.

"Yes, Brother," said Brother Felix. "Follow me, boys." And he began with effort to pick up all four bags.

But Brother Lawrence stopped him. "Let them carry, too." He pushed one bag at Vince and one at me, which left only two for Brother Felix, and the four of us walked to the beds.

Brother Felix said: "Uh, do you wet the bed at night?"

"Why?" Vince said.

"No, sir," I said.

"And your ages?"

But we were gazing around again and didn't respond. I don't know why. I'd heard the question.

"Tell him how old you are!" said Brother Lawrence.

"I'll be ten in November," I said.

"And I'll be twelve in March," Vince said.

"Then you're nine, and you're eleven," said Brother Lawrence, pointing at each of us in turn.

Brother Felix seemed to be waiting in respectful silence. Then he said, gently, "Casey, you will be in the ten-and-below section. And by the way, you're now the youngest one here. Several boys turn ten this month, and Abel Zablonsky will be ten in October."

"Please get on with it, Brother," Brother Lawrence said.

"Yes, Brother. Vince, you will be with the above-tens."

"Can't we be together?" I said.

"On your eleventh birthday we'll transfer you," Brother Lawrence said.

My head did an instant computation, and I felt a door closing on me for a long time. I had not thought of the future at all; I had simply let myself be brought here and left. And now I knew that it would be for far longer than I would ever have thought.

Brother Lawrence gestured with his arms. "Everything at Mount Saint Francis is worked out with a purpose. The dormitory is divided into psychical sections as well as by age." He pointed to an isolated section. "That corner is for bedwetters. Wet your bed once, and you go there with a rubber sheet."

Brother Felix had his head down. Now he raised it and spoke. "Brother, about Blue, uh, Miller: he really should be moved out. He's much too old for the others there."

Brother Lawrence glanced at Vince as he said, "And it has nothing to do with age. There's a fifteen-year-old, several nine-year-olds, and everything in between." Then he turned and, walking away, said, "Miller stays put. You find a drop of piss on even Kurt's mattress, and he goes in, too. No exceptions. And send those two down in ten minutes."

"Come on, boys," said Brother Felix when Brother Lawrence was gone. "I'll show you your beds and lockers."

On the way, I asked Vince so that Brother Felix couldn't hear: "What's that word mean, sounded like physical?"

"Means he's crazy as hell," Vince said.

We unpacked and stowed our clothes in the lockers as fast as we could. Then we went back to Brother Felix's little room, where he had said we should meet him as soon as we were through.

"We say rosary every night," he said. "If you want to lead, you must memorize the mysteries for that day. I'll be walking around to help you if you should get stuck. And if you want to attend morning Mass, tie your towel around the top rail of your bed, and I'll wake you." He hurried the last part, without fully explaining it: "You get five merits for every morning you attend voluntary Mass, and five when you lead rosary. Now, you'd better go on down to Brother Lawrence."

He was waiting for us, twirling his rope so that the cross swung around. When he saw us, he immediately began walking with the obvious understanding that we would follow without having been told. And we did.

We came to a fence and went through a gate to the field. In the distance several brothers and some boys worked at a stoop.

"We do our own work here," Brother Lawrence said. "And there's plenty of extra for those who don't do what they're told." Vince shrugged. "If you goof off, it's more work and demerits. A hundred demerits and you're on the blacklist."

"What's that?" I said.

"No candy. No pool or pinball. No Christmas vacation."

Vince said, "Yeah, but Mother said—"

"You're here now. You'll obey the rules like everybody else."

We walked along for a while without talking, and then we stopped. Brother Lawrence pointed to a fenced-in area. "The regular ponies are kept there," he said, swinging around so that his robe swished. "And over there"—he pointed to a small adjacent field separated from the other one by a wire fence—"are the Shetlands. They have to be kept apart." He made it sound as if we should understand why.

There were white ponies and brown ones; pintos and the stunted Shetlands; black, shaggy ones and sleek, shiny ones.

"Pony boys are assigned every month," he said, and he told us what they did.

"Can we be pony boys?" I said.

"You'll have to get permission from your guardian," Brother Lawrence said. "Have you ever worked with horses before?"

"When we lived in Kentucky we helped take care of a mule," Vince said.

"Mules aren't quite the same thing," Brother Lawrence said.

"We used to ride it, too," Vince said.

"That doesn't mean you know anything about horses," Brother Lawrence said. "There's as much difference between a mule and a horse as there is between a boy and a man. Why a mule?"

"Huh? Our uncle used them in the coal mine."

"You two have a bad habit of saying 'huh' and 'yeah' a lot," Brother Lawrence said, and his jaw muscle rippled slightly. "You worked in the mines?"

"Just helped a little, outside mostly," Vince said.

"Well, you get the permission, then we'll see about it. But you'll take your turn. No special favors. Understand?"

"Yes, Brother," I said. I was anxious to get to the ponies, but he led us back through the fence and a building, into what he called a quadrangle.

As we were crossing the brick courtyard, Brother Lawrence stopped, went to a stone structure, and inspected some bushes growing around it. We followed him. Some were still blooming; most of them were badly wilted. I walked around what was a stone pulpit, well off from a corner of the courtyard. While he seemed to be searching for clues of some kind, I read the tarnished brass plaque, askew but bolted into the face of the pulpit: "Francis, go and repair My house, which you see is falling down." Brother Lawrence looked mad as he led us on to the church.

As he opened one of the huge wooden doors with carvings on them, I was surprised that he had to strain with the effort. Nick and I went in and stood at the back, expecting the headmaster to follow us. But since he stood holding the door, we peeked reverently into the sanctuary, Vince whispered something I didn't understand, and we went back outside.

Brother Lawrence led us down the steps then stopped. "What was all that grabass in there?"

"What?" Vince said.

"You were talking in church," Brother Lawrence told him. "That's five demos."

Vince's face turned red. I knew what it might mean, and I said, "Father Daniels back home reminds me of you."

"Yeah?" Brother Lawrence said. "Vince! You think you're privileged characters, don't you? You think you don't belong here. Well, get this straight: everybody's here for a reason."

※ ※ ※

As we entered the dining hall, all eyes seemed to turn onto us. Brother Lawrence left us standing there and went to the central table where several other brothers sat. Boys in rumpled white jackets carried trays and pitchers to the tables. Brother Felix appeared from one of the boys' tables and escorted us to our seats, five places apart. He then led the blessing, and everybody joined in: "Bless us, oh, Lord, and these thy gifts, which we are about to receive from Thy bounty, through Christ our Lord. Amen."

I looked up once, to find several boys staring at me. When the prayer was over and I was crossing myself, I took the occasion to scratch secretly at my left shoulder, and lost cadence. It made me feel foolish to be finishing a step after the rest of them, and when I looked at the boy on my left I saw that he had not failed to notice. He turned his head slightly, raising his eyebrows, and gave me a goofy smile. But then he continued to make odd facial gestures as he stabbed at his food in quick little spear-like thrusts of his fork. When I reached for the milk pitcher, he pretended to jab at my hand with the fork. I drew back. A fly buzzed above the pitcher, and he caught it quick as a frog. I asked for the other pitcher at my right.

The boy who passed it was eating dejectedly and handed me the pitcher without comment. "I'm Casey," I said, by way of thanks.

"I'm Mickey Rickey," he said sadly. "I'm giving it all to you now so you won't laugh when you hear it later and put them together yourself." He went into a littte one-boy act: "Rickey. Ha-ha! I get it!"

The boys across from me were sort of silent, picking at their food and only glancing at me from time to time. A hand punched me on the left shoulder, and I turned. The one there opened his hand like an offering and displayed a fly, which immediately flew away. I looked at his face, and he opened his mouth. There was a dead fly on his tongue.

I stretched to see Vince, who was talking to a boy next to him. Then I realized that, except for the head table, everybody had been whispering. And that I had been, too.

When the meal was over, we said the other prayer for our "great benefits," and then we rose while the brothers left. When they were gone, the rest of us jammed the doorways until we were all out in the courtyard. Vince and I were to meet Brother Felix by the stone pulpit in ten minutes. I went directly there, then wandered around trying to find Vince, but he didn't show up until after Brother Felix came and took us to our classrooms, where I sat in my desk seat all afternoon after I was introduced as one of the new boys.

Classes dragged on while I thought of nothing much, except who I was and why I was there among strangers. When classes ended I wandered to the recreation room with the others, searching for Vince, talking when I was spoken to but feeling foolish that everybody looked at me. After the evening meal, much like the first one except more solemn, everybody at Mount St. Francis must have gathered around the stone pulpit in the courtyard. I had kept Vince in sight when he left the dining hall ahead of me, and now I went over to him.

He was with a boy. "This is Moon," he said. "That's Casey, my little brother." Then he turned back to Moon. "What's next?"

"We get an hour to screw around out here," Moon said. "Mostly bullshit time. Unless the machine's being oiled."

Vince seemed to know what he meant about the machine, so I didn't ask. I was still bristling over "little brother." He'd never called me that before.

Suddenly a wave of whispering went through the crowd. I felt the boys parting, and I moved with them. Then everybody was looking up, and I followed their eyes. Brother Lawrence was standing above us at the stone pulpit.

He set his jaw, and all went quiet. "Okay, you birds," he said. "Somebody's been pissing on the shrubbery again." He smiled but it was really a frown. "Go right ahead and piss, but when I find you out I'm going to cut your prick off." He looked away, then turned back and added in vicious singsong, "That's the only language you birds seem to understand, so there it is." He gripped the sides of the pulpit. "Now, I have a few other things. First, there was a breakout last night. You know who it was. I know who it was." He let that sink in awhile. "Well, they're back now, but it'll be some time before they can sit easy again." His upper lip seemed to tuck under, stuck, so that his upper teeth shone as he added: "Or eat much. Their places at the table, as you already know, have been taken by the two new boys."

A couple of tall boys moved in front of me, and I couldn't see Brother Lawrence when he said, "The other thing is that there aren't enough of you going to voluntary Mass. If you don't tie your towels on your bed rails, I'm going to have Brother Felix tie them on for you. And from now on the church is going to be closed when services are not being held. Too many of you are going in there to loaf or beat your meat. There'll be a sign on the door to show the hour when you can go in and pray. Pray! Any questions? Anybody feeling especially brave tonight?" I was surrounded by four big boys. "Okay, then. Showers in thirty minutes."

The crowd released me, and I floated around for a while until I found Vince and Moon again. But as I started over to them, two boys came up to me.

"Hey," the stocky one said, "you're the youngest now."

I shrugged.

"Say something," the thin one said. His face was covered with pimples.

"Somethin'," I said.

They laughed. "Hear that?" the thin one said. "Talks like a hillbilly."

"Looks like a dago," the stocky one said. "What's your name?"

"Casey," I said.

"A mick, too," the stocky one said. "A hillbilly-dago-mick."

Vince came over, and Moon walked off. Other boys were gathering.

"Lay off," Vince said.

"Uh-ohhhh," the thin boy said mockingly, rolling his eyes. He pointed to the stocky one. "This is Kenny Clark you're talking to, dago."

Kenny Clark heaved up his pigeon breast.

"I don't care if he's Superman," Vince said. He turned back to Clark. "Leave him a—"

Suddenly Clark reached over and pushed me and I fell across somebody behind me. When I landed, I wrenched around to see Vince land a fist in Clark's face. And then all hell broke loose. I scrabbled around on the bricks and grabbed whatever I could of somebody who was on top of me.

And then they were all gone, except me and Vinny. A brother was swinging his rope at Kenny Clark, who had his hands over his head, running. The brother missed, but he turned and caught the thin boy on the head with a knot. It was like the sound a walnut makes when you crack it just right.

> > >

We lined up with bath towels around us, waiting our turns. It was probably by age, for I found myself with others about as old as I was at the end of a long line. The big boys had been up front and were now returning to their lockers and beds. When Kurt, the biggest boy at the school, passed by without a towel around him, I could see he was a man. He swaggered through the aisles, flipping his wet towel at a boy called Rollo, who had bent over at just the right time. It must have stung like fire, but Rollo didn't yell. He only grabbed his fanny and cried without any sound.

The boy ahead of me had bony wings in his back. Every time he reached back to scratch, they became more pronounced. To have something to do while I waited, I counted the knots in his spine. I was the last one in line. After a while, I saw Vinny walking with Moon back to their beds, and I waved. But he didn't see me. I was on the verge of breaking ranks and going over to say something to him, when Brother Felix came up.

"Here, Casey," he said, handing me a new cake of Lifebuoy soap.

A couple of boys up the line looked around, and I thought one of them smirked.

Brother Felix touched the boy in front of me on the shoulder. "Abel, you're an old man around here. Casey is younger by a month. You must get to know each other."

We shook our heads at each other. All the time, Abel kept trying to get at that itch on his back. When Brother Felix left us and went up to the head of the line, Abel said, "It's that soap he gave you. I wouldn't use it if I was you."

After the last of us had showered and were coming out of the single, large stall, another group of boys had formed a new line. As I passed the rubber sheet section, I realized that they were the bedwetters, going in last, and I determined right then to avoid it over there, no matter what. That night I hit upon the beginning of a scheme which I refined over the next several nights.

Lucky for me, Mother had carefully read the list of required clothing: I had two pairs of pajamas. I would dress for bed in one pair, which I planned to keep unsullied. After rosary, when Brother Felix went to his room and most of the others were asleep or stroking themselves under their covers, I'd go to my locker and change into the bad pair and get the towel I used over and over for padding. Then I'd turn the mattress over when I felt ready for sleep. Other boys got up during the night to go to the bathroom, so I wasn't too conspicuous. I went a few times myself, but no amount of relief would do the trick. There was always enough for the bed. And since I had to be asleep to do it—I could have kept dry only by staying awake all night—it was either deception or the rubber-sheet section.

Something in a dream would usually trigger it: warmth, water, tears—just about anything like that. All I could do was be ready for it when it happened on its own. There was always a connection inside the dream, like a little play I had to finish in bed. And I'd wake up right after or, often, during.

I had no problems with laundry, because we just rolled everything up and chucked it all into a big pile on laundry pick-up day and I never sent out the dirty pajamas and towel. They dried out in my locker during the day. I did think it strange that the brothers could be so short-sighted as to allow the co-mingling of the normal and the...physical laundry. Even the rubber-sheeters threw in their pillow cases and top sheets. At any rate, all of our personal stuff was marked with our locker numbers, and the bed clothes were passed out helter-skelter.

The biggest problem in my system, and the one for whose solution I was constantly groping, was the mattress, because the towel wasn't always enough to keep it dry. That was why I had to wear pajamas in the first place: I needed them as a kind of first filter. But I was real short, so I could just about pick the spot. Since it would be better to do it in the same place over and over, I'd inch way down to the bottom and then I'd ball up and turn at an angle. It was pretty hot down there sometimes, and after a few weeks it didn't smell too good, but some

Lifebuoy chips and peppermint candy helped some. Still, I'd lie down there in my secret nightworld, too scared to move and conscious all the while that at any moment I could be sent to the rubber-sheet section, and I'd wait until I awoke after it was over.

After the entire ordeal, when I had done my locker-rummaging and stowing of the evidence—that is, when dawn came and I finally re-awoke—I could even turn down my covers a little like the other boys. But I'd make a little tunnel, too, so the spot could get some air. And when the guys near me went off to the bathroom, whenever I could I knocked the mattress off the bed, and then flipped it when I put it back on. It got so that I could not always remember at night which side was up; but, if discovered, I was ready at any moment to claim that the mattress must have been used by some old bedwetter before me. (I'd often wrinkle up my nose and point to the wetters' corner.) But I was never found out. The problem went away on its own, just before Christmas.

That first night, as Brother Felix paced the aisles, fingering his rosary, and as I heard a boy intone, "The Fifth Joyful Mystery: The Finding of Our Lord in the Temple," what Brother Lawrence had said earlier resounded like a deep voice within my head: *"You find a drop of piss on even Kurt's mattress, and he goes in, too."* I had not yet perfected the scheme, but when I came back from my locker at the first light of dawn I felt so sure of it that I tied the good towel on the top railing of my bed.

The next morning, after Mass, breakfast, and arithmetic, I was sitting in the front row of religion class, copying into my notebook everything Brother Felix was saying about the divine plan of creation. He had a soothing way of pacing the front of the room, his hands within the opposite sleeves of his robe, and as he turned from the window I saw him see someone in the back of the room. "Good morning, Brother," he said. And then he continued. He was talking about a war in heaven a long time ago.

I heard the voice of Brother Lawrence—"Who was the brightest angel, the one who led the revolt?"—and I thought the question was directed at me since I was unaware of anybody else in the room but the two brothers and myself. I was ready to turn at last to face the music, when I heard another voice.

"Me?" It was the fly boy.

Several boys laughed, and I let out my breath. Then I heard the now familiar sound of rope knot on head, followed by a short cry from the fly boy.

"Yeah, you, wise guy," Brother Lawrence's voice said. "You and Lucifer."

I shrank to my desk as Brother Felix explained that Lucifer meant light, but that he turned into the devil when he fell from heaven and hit earth. After a few minutes I heard the door close and watched Brother Felix walk to the back of the room. I turned. He was comforting the fly boy, who had his head on his desk. The others began to talk and throw things at each other, but Brother Felix didn't stop them right away.

After school, I was to meet Vince in the rec hall after I went to the dorm and got a box of homemade candy from my locker. When I arrived, Kurt was playing pool with a couple of other big boys, several boys were crowded around the pinball machine, and Vince and Moon were playing Ping-Pong, so I sat at a table, put the box of candy on my lap, and began to fiddle with a jigsaw puzzle while I waited for Vince.

I looked over at the pool table. Kurt was getting ready to shoot, pushing the cue stick in and out of the hole made by his left forefinger. Then he jabbed, and scribbed, and the cue ball went flying in the air off the table. I followed it with my eyes, into the hand of Brother Lawrence. He stood by the wall, watching. He chucked the cue ball back to Kurt, saying, "Hey, big guy, you hustling those little fish?"

Kurt raised up and smiled. "I'd play a big fish," he said.

The two boys playing with Kurt smiled and stepped away, one handing Brother Lawrence his cue stick. "Go ahead and play him, Bro," he said.

Brother Lawrence took the stick, Kurt racked the balls, and they shot lags for break. Brother Lawrence won and blasted the triangle of balls, scattering them over the table. But none went in. Vince and Moon stopped playing Ping-Pong and went over to watch. So did the boys playing pinball. So did I.

I held the candy more tightly as Rollo sidled up beside me. It was said that the smell of food could wake him from a deep sleep. Each time Kurt made a ball, the boys cheered; when Brother Lawrence missed, they smiled, but didn't cheer. And when Kurt won, Brother Lawrence said jokingly that it was because Kurt had grown up in a pool room. "And I haven't played since last year, when I beat you." Then he handed the stick to a nearby boy and went out, joking with a couple of younger boys who had taken my place at the table.

Vince came over, and we opened the box. Moon took a piece, and we were eating, when one of the big boys asked for some. Then Kurt had some, and in a few minutes the big boys were digging in for seconds. They pretty well finished it off, taunting Rollo by licking their lips, until he ran out of the room.

Later in the courtyard after the evening meal, Kurt ascended the pulpit and ordered everybody to "Oil the machine!"

The big boys lined up front to back; by roughly tapered heights, the others fell in in front of them. It seemed like they were going to march off in a column, only they were separated from each other by a few feet. Then they spread their legs. Except for the fly boy and Rollo and two shady guys named Blue and Paul standing by on the fringes, only Vince and I were left. Kurt stood near the back of the line.

"Come on back here, guineas," he said, and Vince and I went. "The only rule is, you can't get hit by anybody some part of you ain't under."

There was a murmuring in the ranks, boys yelling, "Send them through the front!" and "Why do they get off?"

But Kurt raised his hands, and they quieted down. Then he directed Vince to get down on his hands and knees and crawl through from the rear, and as he did the big boys slapped at him but not too hard. I moved to the side of the line so I could see better. Vinny picked up speed so that a few missed, but when he came under Kenny Clark, Clark punched him in the side of the face and got in two more on his sides. Vince crawled faster, and by the time he reached the front-end the boys there were too little to crawl under very fast, and not hard hitters. When he crawled under Abel Zablonsky, last in line, he got stuck, raised up, and sent Abel to the ground. Vince was red-faced and breathing hard when he ran back to centerline and gave Clark a push, daring him to fight.

"Knock it off!" Kurt yelled. "Clark, see me when this is over." He laughed as he put his hands on my shoulders, took me to the rear of the line, and urged me to the ground. "Now the little guinea."

I began to crawl through, looking up at the spread legs of the boy who had given the cue stick to Brother Lawrence. Already I had shifted into high gear in my head, but by the time I got going I found that if I slowed entering the next legs, then speeded up when my head was just coming under the next rear-end, I could cause a miss. But even when they hit it wasn't hard, not even Clark's. By the time I got to where Abel had been, he was off to the side, watching.

"That was pretty good, wasn't it, Moose?" Kurt said to the big boy who had been first in line.

While I was getting up, Moose grunted.

Then Kurt whispered to me, "Got any more candy?"

The line was breaking up, the boys milling around, and I whispered back, "We'll be getting some more from home sometime."

"Well,"—he turned to take Vince in, too—"keep in mind what it would be like coming through from the other end, without protection."

That sent Moose into a fit of laughing.

➤ ➤ ➤

We made the midget football team, but I sure didn't like the name. Vince beat out Ken Clark at quarterback, and I made left guard. I got knocked around a lot, but football was my game. One of the biggest thrills was being allowed to attend class in our uniforms on the day of a game. And when we were given Notre Dame's old helmets (some of us stuffed rags inside to keep them from rattling), I felt that I had been presented a golden chalice. Inside was a little blood streak, or what I took for blood, and the smell of long-ago sweat soaked deep into the foam rubber. Each scar on the gold paint seemed to have a history: a dazzling block, a vicious tackle, a grazing cleat. When Vinny discovered J. L. written inside his, we took it as a sign of great things to come for him, for his head became helmeted, on and off the field, in the key battle dress of his hero: Johnny Lujack.

"Florentino," Brother Lawrence said to Vince one day as we were running plays, "you're throwing the ball like a girl. It's got to get there to hit the end cutting across." He tucked his rope and cross out of the way. "Okay, run it again. I'll take quarter. You take end."

Brother Lawrence lifted the hem of his robe and squatted to fit himself under the center. (And he was calling Vince a girl!) When the ball was snapped, I became churning feet, hands gripping my jersey, elbows out and locked, blocking away at my phantom foe; but I was watching for Vinny when he made his cut. And when he did, the ball smashed him in the face.

"You okay?" Brother Lawrence said, but he didn't wait for an answer. "Shake it off, then. Take over."

And Vinny did, licking off a trickle of nose blood.

Hell, I knew what Vince could do. And there wasn't any man in a dress and eyeglasses could do it better.

Vinny called for a huddle and gave the play, same one, and we took our positions. He barked out the signals—"All set, hep, one"—and on "two" the ball was snapped. I turned as Vinny threw his right foot back and, like a dancer, skipped two steps more, then to his right as he gave a little graceful leap off his left leg, his right one bent just right. And the ball spiraled with more than just speed to the flat hands of the end making his cut.

"Now you've got it," Brother Lawrence yelled. "But, you, there!" He was talking to me. "What were you doing all the time?"

I shrugged.

"I want you to take guard-over-center for a while. Your job will be to get the quarterback. If I see you letting up because he's your brother, you'll be sitting on the bench next game." He looked around and pointed to Abel Zablonsky. "Take little Florentino's position. The rest of you over there set up on defense."

The second team moved in around me, and I put up on a four-point stance, digging my cleats in for the charge. I was mad as hell. He had no business calling me "little" to Abel.

Vince broke the huddle and got set behind the center. I looked somewhere between the ball and the center's head. But when Vince called the signals, the center bobbled the ball just as I rammed him with my helmet, which immediately turned sideways on my head. I hit the deck and straightened it up, hearing Brother Lawrence telling the center to "Watch out, son."

Then Lawrence was the center, his robe gathered around his waist and held with his left hand, his right hand on the ball. I was still plenty mad, but I noted the black britches he wore, as I saw Vince's hands move in uncertainly under the huge crotch. Vince called the signals, the ball snapped up, and I was off. But nothing stopped me, and I broke into the backfield at the same time that Vince turned to give a handoff. With the momentum, I had no choice: I knocked what I considered to be the holy shit out of my brother.

But it must really have been out of myself. I saw stars the entire time I heard Lawrence say, "Okay! Not bad at all," then proceed to tell us that we had to be able to go both ways on this team, that it wasn't enough just to throw or block or run. He didn't want any offensive stars, not unless they could block and tackle, too. You had to be a defensive man to make his team.

❧ ❧ ❧

I could sit in the rec room fairly undisturbed if I set out on the table a box of candy from home. And I didn't have to worry about everybody taking some; only Kurt and Moose and the other big boy ate it while they played pool. The other guys left it, and me, alone. So after I had been there a couple of weeks, I got all set with school stationery and pencil, and I wrote my first letter home:

Mt. St. Francis School

Sept. 20, 1947

Dear Mother,

Just a few lines to let you know that we are very well and hope that everybody at home is the same. Do you get home very much from Richmond?

My average in spelling is ninety-nine. I am the highest one in class. I do not know about Vinny, but I guess he is o.k. We are both doing good in everything.

Sometimes the Brother gives us a little speech in the courtyard from his stand. I guess we need it sometimes too. But he isn't too tough on us so don't worry too much.

We get to ride the ponies sometimes. Can't we be pony boys?

I went to confession the other day, so I'm still in the state of grace I guess.

We got your letter with the good news, and we are glad to know that we are going to get a package. Yours are good too, but I hope it will be some candy from home because it is so good.

I wonder how Rosie and Aunt Gabriella and Grandmother all are at home.

Well closing now.

Your loving son,

Casey F.

I went over my words again and again, closing up a few loops while admiring my cursive handwriting. When some of the boys headed to the dorm for shower time, I went along, whisper-whistling a catchy tune. As we walked through the door of the dorm, Clark was on his way down the stairs, excited. He stopped Kurt and Moose and some of the others, and we all froze, hushed, to see what was up.

"He's coming down for kitchen duty!" Clark whispered.

Kurt gave orders, and Clark went up again. The rest of us hid in the bottom stairwell. There were maybe fifteen of us. While we were waiting, Mickey Rickey came in the door, and Kurt motioned him over and added him to the rest of us he was holding there with his arm out.

After a while, a thump sounded above, then scraping. Somebody yelled up there, and then one of the boys with us started to go. But Kurt wouldn't let him yet.

Suddenly, somebody was screaming and running the last flight of stairs, and Kurt led us out. When the tall, gaunt figure on the stairs saw us, his face, which looked like Lincoln's, went frantic; and he tried to turn, but Clark was on his back, grabbing the railing and sending him on. Then Clark grabbed his hair and jerked his head back, and Blue fell into the crowd at the bottom. There, Kurt had him. Then they all had him. Clark put his fist in Blue's mouth and kept his head up. The mob kept the rest of him up, so he couldn't even fall. As the hands reached up to him, it appeared that they were passing his head around. They did not hit the face.

Later, after my nighttime routine, as I lay at the bottom of my bed awaiting the inevitable, sleep did not come. So neither did the other. And then Brother Felix was walking the aisles for wake-up for voluntary Mass. I had my dirty towel under me, the good one still back in the locker, but I wanted those five merits. And I had to pray, officially, that Brother Lawrence wouldn't find out about what we'd done to Blue. I hadn't touched him, maybe because I hadn't been able to reach him. But I was still in on it, and I knew it. So I tied the dirty towel by my rosary on the rail, and I waited. Just as I heard Brother Felix approaching, I untied it and whispered to him that I was already awake. When he left, I knocked my mattress off and turned it, then went to my locker when no one was looking and did what I had to do there.

The church was a domed, marble cavern several boys and I entered with echoes. I dipped into the holy water and was crossing myself, when Vince and Moon came up behind me, breathing hard. The three of us went to the third pew from the front, genuflected, and knelt behind the other boys. The brothers were already there, front pew. I opened my Missal to the prayers to prepare for Mass, then began searching out every indulgence I could find, saying to myself, between searches, Don't let him find out about Blue, oh, Lord, when the others rose and I went up with them.

Rollo came out like a nervous cherub in his black cassock and white, lacy surplice, leading the little priest—the boys called him Father Shorty—and carrying the Book like a platter. Moon punched Vince and whispered, "The fat fuck's going to eat the Book," and we stifled laughs. At the foot of the altar they genuflected, went up to altar level, genuflected there, and set up the table. Father Shorty had to use a small riser. When they descended and the priest genuflected while Rollo knelt, the rest of us stayed down with Rollo, and the opening prayers began.

One good thing about daily Mass: there was no sermon. A fast priest could knock off the entire thing—from opening prayers at the foot of the altar to the final blessing—in maybe twenty minutes, flat. This one was setting a record. We were at the Communion rail in fifteen minutes, and as Rollo turned with the Paten after receiving the Host, I thought I'd bust out laughing when I saw him wolfing it down like a cookie. But I managed to make myself sufficiently penitent, as I closed my eyes and stuck out my tongue to receive. I then closed my mouth and bowed my head, and the old miracle came back as it always had at this moment: I had received the body of Christ. All my sins were wiped away.

Except as I returned to the pew and knelt and bowed there, I knew that you had to have made a good Confession for it to be so. I had not confessed at all since last night's mauling of Blue, and while I tried to rationalize my role in it, telling myself that I had not actually participated, I knew that I had in some serious way. I had not resisted the temptation to watch; I had not tried to stop it. But then I raised my head and opened my eyes, seeing several of those in front of me who had been an active part of the mob, and I felt better. Let Blue get all right, I thought, and I said an *Our Father*, a *Hail Mary*, and a *Glory Be* for him. I added what I tried to will into a retroactively perfect Act of Contrition for myself and then dug around for some indulgences not of just days, but years.

After the priest finished The Last Gospel, then gave us his blessing and said, "*Ite, missa est*," and Rollo led him off, we left the pew and made the long walk back through the center aisle. By the time we crossed ourselves I had ejaculated four times, solemnly, internally, the little mother lode of a one-liner once printed in red on my sweat-stained and all-but-disintegrated scapular, barely attached to and hanging from the now gray ribbon-string around my neck, like a little clump of holy lint: *Lord, have mercy on me, a sinner.*

We were on the steps, when Brother Luke, who taught arithmetic and worked in the dining hall, caught up with us. "You each get five demerits for laughing in church," he said with his hands in his sleeves. He didn't even stop.

My soul sank. Vince looked like he'd been lassoed from behind the way he halted.

"Told you," Moon said to Vince. "Stay the hell away from church. It's nothing but trouble."

I was hurt and reeling, but at least I'd be able to go safely alone from now on.

Mt. St. Francis School

Sept. 30, 1947

Dear Mother,

Just a few lines to let you know we received your letter and were very glad to hear from you.

Our clothes from you got in but they are over at the laundry getting marked. We got a package from home with candy, and is it good. Nobody around here ever had any so good so we give a little to some of the boys ever now and then.

We just got through riding the ponies and do they go fast. Vince and me went together and took them as fast as they could go. We even gave them a piece of the candy. Why can't we be pony boys?

How come you don't really want us to play football? Well, it's over now anyway.

Sunday we had a contest. It was between two teams blue and gold. We had broad jumping, football passing, kicking, and cake eating contest. Vinny won a ribbon. Then each boy got a piece of cake and we tried to see who could eat it the fastest. The one who ate it fastest whistled and won the prize. I almost won that one but not quite. We are going to have a party Friday.

With love,

Casey

P.S. I signed up to serve daily mass for a week. I get 10 merits every time.

Vince and Moon piled up the demos and had to peel potatoes and work as servers in the dining hall. Brother Felix let me work with him in the dispensary, which came in handy when I picked up a cold sore and got kicked in the nose in football. Another time, I had chapped lips so bad they bled. Brother Felix had to consult a doctor by telephone to find out what to do.

As he swabbed my lips with a cotton-tipped stick, dipping it into a small bottle, I asked him what it was. "Tastes sweet."

"It ought to," he said. "It's called saccharin, many times sweeter than sugar."

"How can something sweet help?" I said. I had always thought medicine had to hurt or stink, or both.

"It just naturally cures," he said, as he finished and then took out a little tin of snuff from under his robe. He pinched a bit and took it in the nose, and his nostrils dilated. He could have inserted a nickel into each one.

Then he let me try a few grains, and I sneezed. But it tasted—or smelled; I couldn't tell which—pretty good.

While I was sweeping up and putting the place to order, he told me that I was a good helper. He called me Cosimo.

"I don't like that name, Brother Felix," I said. "Please call me Casey."

"Why, you mustn't be ashamed of your name," he said. "You have such a pretty one." He said it all: "Cosimo Florentino."

"There's a middle one, too," I said.

He smiled. "What is it?"

"Promise you won't tell?" I said.

"Promise," he said.

"Boggs," I said.

We both laughed.

"It was somebody's last name back home," I said. "I think he was a man my daddy knew."

"What do you remember about your father?" he said.

"Not much," I said.

"Do you know where he is?" he said.

"Huh-uh, Brother," I said. I wanted to get off the subject. "So call me Casey, will you, Brother Felix?"

"Sure," he said. "But you should know that your last name makes you a namesake of one of the greatest cities in the world—Florence, Italy."

"Really?" I said.

"Yes," he said. "And it means Little Flower. One of our greatest saints was called The Little Flower. She was Saint Thérèse of Lisieux."

I didn't exactly like being named after a woman on top of everything else, but when he told me about her I was kind of proud—at least now of my last name.

And while I was feeling the effects of my new knowledge, Brother Felix said without explanation, "You must pray for Brother Lawrence, Casey. Will you offer the rosary for him tonight?"

I started to ask him why he needed one. I was still trying to remember Blue, but he had disappeared and it was harder to pray for them when they weren't around unless they were family, almost as hard as for the faceless souls in Purgatory we were always being reminded to remember. That night, though, after group rosary, which I dedicated to my usual hierarchy of relatives and to the Purgatorians Brother Felix always invoked near the end, while I was biding my time in my nocturnal secrecies I said a whole extra rosary—speedily, I admit. I figured Blue had gone back to his home and that whatever prayers had reached their mark, had worked. So I gave Lawrence a decade, started to take one for myself but remembered Aunt Gabie's born-dead baby in Limbo (though I couldn't pray him out), and gave the rest to Vinny. He must have been racing Moon to the blacklist. And they were about halfway there.

Mt. St. Francis School

October 11, 1947

Dear Mother,

Just a few lines to let you know that we are well and hope you are the same.

We got a letter from Father Daniels and he said we had his catcher's mit. Now that you have moved back home would you tell him that we don't have it? But tell him that we will be sending the first baseman's mit tomorrow.

We didn't know Cousin Janet Faye was over at Madonna Vista. She just wrote us and said she couldn't make it this week but she would come over next week.

Football's over so you don't need to worry about it. We're going out for basketball next. But we'd really like to be pony boys. Can't we???!!

They sure can't make good spaghetti here.

Well I'll close for now.

With love,

Vinny & Casey

He said to sign his name too.

P.S. Send us some more money and candy as it is running out.

On November 10, I would *be* 10: a coincidence of numbers that wanted a special celebration. It was the one above all others I had been waiting for, when I would be able at last to write my age in two digits. The days were sunny but colder, the bushes around the pulpit had pretty much dried out, and now only a few dead leaves blew across the courtyard in the chill air.

As I came out of the dormitory, huddled in my mackinaw on my way to the rec room, I stopped as I so often did to read the tilted plaque on the pulpit: "Francis, go and repair My house, which you see is falling down." I looked around to see if anyone was watching, and I tried to straighten it but the holes were too big. I went to the back of the pulpit. Hidden by the steps, but accessible, was a small rectangular opening at the bottom that led inside the pulpit, and I thought that from inside the bolts could be tightened to set the plaque even.

Suddenly, I heard voices and jumped off the step and pretended to be looking at the dried bushes. I needn't have worried. It was only Carroll Stanley, the school pretty boy, walking with a visitor. They said he was in for stealing a car, but he never paid any attention to any of us. Blond and well-built, he strutted like a cheerleader. His aloofness was different from Rollo's or Paul's or Moon's or poor old Blue's; they were just scared or sorrowful. Everything about Stanley said that he was too good for the rest of us, and Kurt had tried from time to time to knock him down a peg or two. But it was also known that Stanley was Brother Lawrence's favorite, and you didn't mess around with somebody like that. He ran the hundred in twelve-plus and was probably going into the trophy room in the dorm building to show off his awards to his visitor, who, I now saw, was a girl with long hair, blowing in the breeze.

They had descended the steps of the administration building, and I went all the way up to the platform of the pulpit and peered over the solid stone railing. Her coat was bright green, open and showing a pleated yellow dress. The sound of her high heels on the cobblestones echoed strangely into the pulpit enclosure. Every few steps she took there was a scuffing sound, as if she was wearing them for the first time. But she was older than Carroll, that was plain.

And then she laughed. I had forgotten that feminine sound so completely, it sent a shiver through me. I wanted to make myself known to them, and almost did, as I stood openly and watched him take her where I thought he would. I left the pulpit then and went to the rec room.

Kurt, Moose, and the other big boy were not playing pool; three others were, and three waited their turn. The pinball machine was singing away with bells and bumps, and a loud Ping-Pong game was in progress. Vince and Moon were sitting on the floor in a corner, and I went over.

"Hi, Vinny," I said.

Vince looked a hello but didn't speak. He was in a thick conversation with Moon. I sat on the floor beside him and leaned against the wall.

"Look," Moon said to Vince, "I don't want you to go on the blacklist, too, but when you do that's when we make our break." Suddenly he seemed to notice me for the first time. "You didn't hear that, piss head."

"Watch it, Mullins," Vince said. "He's okay."

That seemed to be enough, and Moon laughed wickedly. "I'm going home for Christmas, buddy, blacklist or no blacklist. If you think you can balance demos by peeling spuds till then, go right ahead. But just wait: Brother Four-Eyes'll come up with something."

"I'm still going to try it legit," Vince said. "I don't even have to be here, you know."

That sent Moon into a silent rage. He jumped up and left.

But Vince didn't talk to me. He just sat there as if he harbored some secret grudge.

"Just how many demos you got?" I said after a while. I had ninety merits. As soon as I had asked, I felt like the little egghead who, safe with his 99, had just asked the class dunce what he had made.

Vince's eyes and mouth registered disgust for me. He got up and went to watch pinball.

I thought I'd write a letter, but I didn't have any candy, Kurt and his buddies weren't there to keep the table quiet for me anyway, and the cage where we drew stationery was closed. So I left the rec room and headed back to the dorm. Rollo was lurking around the pulpit, and before I knew it I yelled at him. He started to run, and I told him to stop. Then I went up to him.

"What you chewing?" I said.

He swallowed whatever it was and said, "Nothing. Leave me alone."

"Give me some," I ordered.

His mouth drooled. He reached around and unstuck his pants in the rear, breaking his legs to adjust, I supposed, what was rumored to always be back there. He must have seen my face give away what I'd just thought, because he went wild, dancing in place as if the cobblestones were hot coals. Before I realized what was happening, he had me by the neck and was dragging me behind the pulpit. "You want something, you wop? Here!" And he moved my mackinaw aside and bit me through the shirt on the shoulder.

I might have fainted in that moment of pain. It was as if a bear was mauling me and that if I cried out, I was done for. I'd gone limp in his arms; he had to hold me to keep me up. With the pain shooting through my shoulder, I was made to smell the truth about the rumor that Rollo was worse than just a bed-wetter. And he was awake.

I had one squashed piece of seafoam candy, and I managed to get it out of my pocket as he released me. "Here!" I said. "Take it." I was crying silently and rubbing my shoulder, but I was afraid to do much more.

He downed it like tablet, then said, "This all you got, you little—"

Flower, I thought.

"—prick?" he said. He could see it was. "You're all name. Nobody can't even say it."

"I'll get more from home," I said, choking the words out.

"Good," he said. He was changed. "And if you tell Kurt, I'll bite you're head off." He trotted off cockily.

I thought at first that I should go to the dispensary, but if Brother Felix was there he'd want to know who had done it. So I sucked my nose and damn near broke my neck trying to see the place. Teeth marks made a purplish wound on the point of my shoulder, where there wasn't enough flesh to grab. I dragged myself to the pulpit platform, where behind its sides I sat until the last snuffle. The rectangular opening seemed inviting, a place to hide, but I rose and went to the dorm.

I was so shaken that I avoided the immediate stairs and continued down the corridor to the back ones. That way I would come up in the rear of the dorm, nearer my locker. As I turned the corner, I saw Brother Lawrence, bent looking through the keyhole to the trophy room. He saw me, too, and as he rose he tripped slightly on his robe and hurried toward me on the balls of his feet, ordering me in a loud whisper to "Get up to the dormitory, now!"

I turned and ran to the front stairs, and up, hearing him go out the front door.

I went straight to the window. He was walking fast across the courtyard, glancing over his shoulder. When he looked up, I ducked and stayed down a long moment. Then I peeked, just as he was going up the steps to the administration building.

I went to my locker, but I didn't know why. There was nothing in it for shoulder bite. I thought I'd lie down, but it was against the rules. You could only go to the dorm to get something from your locker or to change clothes for sports. Then why had he ordered me here? Why hadn't he asked me why I was there in the first place? And what had he been looking at?

I went down the back stairs and creeped through the hallway. If anyone came along, I'd go to the dispensary. If Brother Felix was there, I'd tell him a pony bit me; if he wasn't, I'd open the door with my key and find something to put on the shoulder. At the trophy room I heard voices and knelt with my eye to the keyhole. I saw Kurt and the big boy whose name I didn't know, but not much else. Their attention was focused down, and I raised my head for the angle, bumping the doorknob.

The door flew open silently, and I was jerked inside. "I told you I heard somebody before," the big boy whose name I didn't know said.

"What do you want, Elgin, a blue ribbon?" Kurt said.

Carroll was lying on his side on the floor across the room. His hands were tied behind his back. That's all I could see of him. He didn't move.

Kurt stood aside. "This what you want to see, little guinea?"

The large, bare ass of Moose churned and thrust off to the right, where I could see beneath him the struggling girl. She lay on the big boys' coats; her yellow dress and green coat were neatly placed on a chair. So were her underclothes.

"Jesus," Elgin said, "ain't she something?"

When Moose finished, he rolled off, and I saw that she was gagged. He had held her arms down, and now she moved as if to rise, trying to cover her breasts and at the same time reaching for the gag. A muffled sound came from her mouth; her eyes were wide with delirium. She wasn't just a girl.

Kurt pointed at her, sternly, and she sat still, her head bowed so that her hair fell forward. Her crying became louder, as she pulled a coat across her, then pulled all the coats over her. Her muffled moaning was terrible to hear.

"I'm going again," Elgin said.

She suddenly thrashed beneath the coats.

"Let her go, Kurt," I said. "I've got lots of candy coming from home. I'll get anything you want."

"Stay put, Elgin," Kurt said. "You want a little feel, Florentino?"

"Nah, that's okay," I said. "Come on, let her go."

"I want to go again," Elgin said.

Moose had risen, pulled his pants up, and said, "Me, too."

"Damnit, me, too," Kurt said. "But we better not. Something might happen to her."

"You shitting me?" Moose said. "She could take on a army."

"She's been around," Kurt said. "But that's enough." He went over to Carroll and knelt down beside him, taking out of his pocket a little white tube. He broke the tube, rolled Carroll to face him, and put the tube under his nose.

Carroll woke up, shaking his head violently. He tried to get up, but Kurt held him down with a hand. "Now, listen, stud," Kurt said, "I'm only going to say this once. When we leave, you and your sister get dressed back up all nice and pretty. Use the criggy...uh, pahdon me, the bawthroom, across the hall. If a word of this gets out, you'll wish your tongue was cut out. And it will be, along with your prick."

"Yeah, if he's got a prick," Elgin said.

Moose laughed, too, but they were both mad that they couldn't go again.

Kurt walked to the coats. "You hear that?" he said.

She nodded her head so that it could be seen.

"When you leave here, go right on out the gate with that pretty little car of yours," Kurt said. "We'll be watching to see that you do. And if word gets back that you've blown the whistle, pretty boy here's a goner."

"Let's just go with her," Elgin said.

"Hell, let's take the car," Moose said.

"We'll leave when the time's right," Kurt said. "We ain't cooled off from before we got here, only Lawrence don't know that." Then he looked at me. "You can go on now, but, hey!"

I was watching the coats; I turned to him.

"I don't have to tell you what I just told this homo, do I?" He pointed at Carroll.

I shook my head.

"Do I?" he said.

"Hell, no," I said.

"Okay, then," he said. "And, listen. Get me some more of these from the dispensary." He showed me the broken white tube.

"What is it?" I said.

"Have a sniff," he said, and he stuck it under my nose, sending me from the room with my head spinning.

Since Kurt, Moose, and Elgin were the only boys their size at St. Francis, they had no teams to play on except for track, where Moose pushed the shot-put like a cannon ball; Elgin sent the discus sailing as on air; and, after a dazzling run, muscles rippling, Kurt hurled the javelin from his perfectly canted body. It always stuck, far down the field.

But those three had no regard for what they called basketball: pussyball. The closest they came to it was hanging around the gym during off-hours and using the balls to wallop those they ordered against the wall. They called it dodge ball, like the game; but once, when they got going on Paul and Moon, the others of us watched as those two slow ones could do nothing more than cover their heads and turn their backs while the balls blasted them. Kurt let them go after the fun, and then somebody found Rollo and put him up for the rest of us.

Lawrence drilled us more patiently in basketball than he had in football: quick dribbles, crisp passing, soft lay-ups, which he called a crips. He showed us the right touch, all in the fingertips. He was a wicked set-shot himself and seemed to be looking for an heir to his skill. He spent hours with me and Vinny, trying to give us the secret. There was no rancor, no set-up plays where he pitted us against each other. He was interested in tucked elbows, ten fingertips under the ball, eyes fitted just behind, and a smooth push with a jump off the balls of the feet.

But he also wanted distance, and that I could not give him. He relied on Vinny for that. So I became point guard—a pretty good passer—and fed Vinny whenever he was open.

Mt. St. Francis School

October 30, 1947

Dear Mother,

Just a few lines to let you know we received your letter and were very glad to hear from you.

Cousin Janet Faye called up here and they told us she said she could come over next week not this. Uncle Pasco might be over to take us to a ball game.

You should have seen our first basketball game today. We beat this one team 15 to 6!!!!! Vinny made lots of crips, and I made a foul shot.

We're still riding the ponies and we won't take them so fast anymore. But can't we really be pony boys? They like us a lot better than the ones taking care of them now.

We sent the first baseman's mit, but you tell Father Daniels we still don't have his catcher's mit.

I just now made a hundred in spelling, one boy made thirty, and I'm writing this in class.

Brother Lawrence buys stamps to mail the letters with so we don't have to buy them. We don't even have to lick the envelopes. He does that for us too when he collects it all for the mail.

Pretty soon it will be lunch time so I will be closing.

Love,

Casey (and Vinny)

P.S. Vinny said Cousin Janet Faye sent us a quarter, but you'd better send some too as it is running out. Tell Aunt Gabie to send seafoam next time. I lost one pair of my pajamas. Could you send one more for my birthday?

▸ ▸ ▸

After what happened to Carroll and his poor sister, I felt bad being around Lawrence on the basketball court, and once he sat next to me on the bus when we played away. He went out of his way to make me feel special. But I didn't like it. Mainly because Vince and the other boys didn't like it. I felt like a little jerk every time I lost the ball or double-dribbled or walked and Lawrence yelled, "That's all right. Shake it off." And I didn't make a single point in the next three games, but Lawrence kept me on the first team. A couple of other guys were by then clearly better than I was, and after a while pretty much the whole team was down on me.

But I didn't care as much about that as I did about the other. I was so scared of what might happen, I hadn't even told Vinny what Kurt and them had done.

> *Mt. St. Francis School*
>
> *November 11, 1947*
>
> *Dear Mother,*
>
> *We received your letter and was very glad to hear from you.*
>
> *I was sick in bed but now I am all right. There was another boy sick in his bed too. His name is Paul and I tried to talk to him. But he wouldn't do it. I don't know what was wrong with him.*
>
> *The other day Uncle Pasco and Freddy came up to see me when I was sick. They took Vinny to a ball game. We are all going to the zoo next Sunday if all goes well they said.*
>
> *I got the house shoes but they are too little so I am not wearing them. I'll take them back when I go home for Christmas. I want to go home for Christmas. So does Vince. The pajamas sure do come in handy.*
>
> *I made A in everything but history.*
>
> *Well, I'll close for now.*
>
> Love,
>
>   *Casey (and Vinny)*

Mother still had not given us permission to be pony boys, and I was thinking about asking Lawrence to let me be one without it. But I knew what I would be trading off, and I didn't. Vince didn't even ride them much anymore. When I went to the stables to check out one for a ride around the path, I could tell the ponies were pleased to see me. They'd been cooped up all day by two boys who didn't really seem to care that much about the job. So I'd ride as many of them as I could, figuring they needed the exercise. When I was on the path, I'd give them some candy or something. I even tried rubbing some saccharin on their lips, but they didn't much care for it.

When I thought one was my friend, I'd gallop at full speed, bent over with my arms around it, smelling the intoxicating aroma from its mane. Even the Shetlands liked the attention, to a point, although I couldn't rub them the way I could the pintos. They'd balk and run around in little circles, grunting and snorting, like big dogs. Once, when one of them made a puny rear and I laughed, it tried to bite me when I offered it a piece of bread.

But there was never any doubt about Queenie.

We were all out in the courtyard one day, when the crowd began to part and a gradual silence descended all around. Lawrence was leading a procession of some sort, and I maneuvered for a better view. Behind Lawrence two boys held each side of the halter of a beautiful palomino, almost fully grown. The hollow clopping of horseshoes sounded on the cobblestones, as Lawrence led the horse through the boys and walked up the steps to the pulpit.

"This is Duchess," he said. "She was a show pony given to Mount St. Francis by the Big Brother Organization. She'll be kept in a separate stall and pastured in her own field. I don't want any other horse to get near her, and she's not for riding." He smiled lewdly. "Not any kind of riding."

I kept my eyes on her. She was larger than any horse there, her colors a variation of tans. Except for her tail and mane. They were fine golden hairs, like something spun, and they shone in the sun like beams. Her flesh quivered and she snorted, then shook her long neck so that music came from her harness. Then she let go a pile, everybody laughed, and the boys holding her moved her to the other side.

"Where's Casey?" Lawrence shouted.

The crowd around me showed him, and he called me to the steps at the back of the pulpit.

"Come on up here," he said, and I walked the steps to the platform of the pulpit. "She'll be yours to take care of, but you won't be able to ride her after today."

He motioned to the two boys, and they brought her around. I gauged the distance to her back which, without a saddle, was too great; and then Lawrence had me by the waist and lifted me on. Her long tail swished to the side, touching my leg, as her head turned back. She seemed to want to know who I was.

I looked down at one of the boys holding her bridle and told him flatly to give it to me. Then I walked her off while all of them stepped back and reached out to touch her. The rhythmic clopping set up a pacing in my head, as I moved with each stride of her beneath me. The drag of her shoes before each clop suddenly stopped, and I was sure that she wanted to gallop away, as I did. As I approached the far side of the courtyard, out of earshot, I bent over as far as I could. I wanted to tell her something, but I didn't know what. Finally, I whispered as sweetly as I could, "Duchess—." It didn't sound right. "You're all mine, Queenie."

▸ ▸ ▸

I wasn't really Queenie's pony boy. I was just in charge of cleaning her stall and things like that. But it was enough. When I was finished, I could watch her as she idled in the pasture and, occasionally, broke out in a short burst of speed, her tail out and head thrust forward, drinking wind. In the movies, glossy, ebony stallions rose majestically on their hind feet, whinnying and pawing the air; I wanted to be there when Queenie reared like that. But she stayed near the far fence most of the time, and I had to walk a long way to see her close. She kept her back turned. When I approached her, she looked across the fence with big, sad eyes, pawed the ground, and walked off. Still, I was certain that she was the only one of all the others that could rear in the way I thought it should be done.

Mt. St. Francis School

November 13, 1947

Dear Mother,

Just a few lines to let you know we are both well and hope that everybody at home is the same.

We got a new pony but she is too good for us to really ride.

We sure were surprised to see Father Daniels here. He gave us the envelopes. And he said to just forget the catcher's mit. We already forgot it because we never did take it. Anyway, the envelopes will come in handy because there is always something to buy here.

I was going to ask Father to send me a black cassock because the one I serve Mass in here is too big. But I forgot. But now I guess I'll be coming home soon so I'll just wait.

For Christmas we get some presents and we are going to have a party. I cannot wait to get home for Christmas. Vinny can't either. But the brothers are real good to us.

Uncle Pasco didn't come and take us to the zoo. And Cousin Janet Faye didn't come too.

Well, closing now.

With love,

Casey

My turn was coming up again for serving morning Mass, and I could not take Communion one more time without confessing. I had put it off for as long as I could; and then, on a Saturday evening, I found myself waiting in line by the confessional at the side aisle of the church, examining my conscience like an auditor. I had made a bad confession after the incident with Blue—a double sin, since I still hadn't confessed the original—and now because I had been a witness I was involved in the terrible deed with Carroll's sister. Then, last Saturday night, I had drunk water after midnight, breaking my fast, then pretended to myself that I hadn't as I took Communion the next morning. What I had accumulated in so short a time amounted to sacrilege, and there wasn't much worse than that. So I was heavy-hearted as I waited, trying to find the right words.

I had heard that Carroll Stanley had left St. Francis, some said with his sister that day, in her car. But others said they'd seen him after that. Whatever the truth, I hadn't seen him in a couple of days, and I feared the time when he might return with the law and take us all in—Kurt and his buddies, and me, and maybe even Lawrence. Brother Felix had told me to pray for him, even before I'd caught him at the keyhole; and I had, sort of. Maybe Brother Felix knew more about him than even I did.

Abel Zablonsky—with surely only venial sins—came from the confessional, and I went in. I knelt, crossed myself, and said, "Bless me, Father, for I have sinned. It has been two weeks since my last confession. I have talked, laughed, and looked around in church." It was my standard opening, probably everybody else's, too. But back home there weren't any demos attached to such deeds, only a few *Hail Mary*s. I was thankful to Holy Mother Church that she wouldn't let her priests give away what they heard in here, but I wasn't sure about bigger stuff at St. Francis yet.

"How many times, my son?" The priest's voice came through the screen like a movie father's question.

"Three times, Father," I said.

"Go on," he said, kindly.

"I took three apples from the dining hall," and, before I could check myself, I added, "three times."

"So that's nine apples, yes?"

I nodded my head, then realized that he couldn't see. "Yes. Father."

"And did you eat the apples, or did you...sell them?"

"I gave them to a horse, Father." He pretended to clear his throat, but I heard the chuckle.

"Is there more, my son?"

I always waited till the end for this next one: "I had impure thoughts—." I hesitated, thinking of Carroll's poor sister, then said, "one time."

He asked me if that was all, and I said that it was.

"Say a good Act of Contrition."

I said the prayer while he muttered my absolution in Latin, but I could feel in my bones that it was imperfect. Then he gave me a smaller penance than I thought he should and told me to "Go and sin no more."

For whatever reason I left the confessional feeling guiltier and more heavy-hearted than before I had gone in.

, , ,

Then Paul stole Queenie and ran away.

The news spread throughout the dining hall one morning, and during the day, as I sat numbly through classes, praying that it was just one of the many lies always spreading around. Between classes, the two boys on the basketball team who had a justifiable grudge against me said things like, "Lose your horse?" and "Paul's probably sold it for glue by now." At recess, Rollo came up and whispered, "I bet that fucked-up Paul's hosing that nag." I had to wait all day to find out the truth. When I went to her stall, then searched the field, she wasn't there at all.

After several days of jibes and torment, during which I made innumerable pacts with God, Saint Jude, and the BVM, I stumped into the dining hall for the evening meal. The boys at my table had at last tired of their horse-and-Paul jokes, and as we took our seats Mickey Rickey, Abel Zablonsky, and even the fly boy all went into a silent stare at one another. We said the prayer; and then as Vince, Moon, and the other servers brought out the food and we ate, I saw Lawrence at the head table motion to two brothers near the coat room. He stopped eating, stood up, and walked around the table to the center of the room. The two brothers stepped into the coat room, and came out with Paul.

They led him to Lawrence, and Lawrence waved the brothers away. We all put down our forks, like a clicking drum roll. Those who faced away from the center turned their chairs. All the time Paul looked straight at Lawrence.

Lawrence slapped him. "This turd has stolen." He slapped him again. "In the middle of the night he took the new pony and sold it to the first sap he could find." He turned to all of us, but it seemed only to me. "He was on his way to California."

As Lawrence turned back to Paul, I saw Brother Felix look at Brother Luke and shake his head sorrowfully. Lawrence slapped Paul again, and Paul smiled, and then Lawrence hit him in the face with both fists at the same time. Brother Felix rose and began to walk around to the front. Paul staggered, but righted himself, and gave Lawrence a look of defiance. "He must have had some time," Lawrence said. "It looks like he picked up a case of syph along the way." And then Lawrence hit him with his knotted rope again and again until Brother Felix and two other brothers moved in. "Yes," Lawrence said, "get him away from me."

The next day was longer than the one when I had heard about Paul stealing Queenie, because late the night before, just before rosary, I heard that Queenie was back. That gave me a night of, at least, dry sleeplessness. It gave me twenty decades of rosary beads, too. I had to wait all the next day until classes were over, and then I ran to the pasture. Before I saw her, I knew she was there. The whinny could not have come from any of the others.

That evening Kurt oiled the machine from the pulpit. We stood straddle-legged, waiting to see who would go through, and in a few minutes Elgin and Moose came from the dorm with Paul. They put him through the front, and when his face came under my legs I landed a token blow, then turned to watch as he crawled on to the cocked fists held high in the air. Kurt now stood at the head of the line, facing us, and as Paul rose Kurt slapped him with one hand and hit him full in the stomach with the other. Two boys caught him, and Kurt broke an ammonia tube under his nose. When he revived, Kurt said, "Okay, take him up to his rubber sheet." He pointed to a couple others. "You two, go keep Fairy Felix busy with some sob story. Any one will do."

Later, when we were on the second sorrowful mystery during rosary, Brother Felix stopped at my bed and bent down. I was still in my respectable pajamas, so it couldn't be that. "Put on your robe and go down and open the dispensary. Wait for me there. If anyone questions you, tell him you have my permission." I started to ask him if that included Brother Lawrence, as he said again, "*Anyone.*"

At my locker I put on the too-little house shoes and my new bathrobe with a yellow rope for a belt. By the time I went to the dispensary, near the trophy room, my feet were hurting, and I took off the shoes. Then I took several tubes of ammonia, put them in my pocket, and sat down. The second sorrowful mystery came to mind, and I continued in my head where I had left off.

It wasn't long before Brother Felix came in, helping Paul.

I wondered immediately if Paul knew that I had hit him, and I wanted to tell him that I had only because Kurt and his buddies were watching, that I was sorry. But I figured Paul knew a faked hit from a real one by now; besides, he wasn't in any shape to listen to any apology from me.

As Brother Felix led him to my chair, I rose to get the gauze and scissors and iodine and whatever else I thought was needed. Brother Felix called for gauze pads and a pan of warm, soapy water; and I mixed it in the way I had seen him do it so often, dropping in a bit of the hygienic soap, then running the water into it. Brother Felix then came to the sink and, like a doctor, washed his big, hairy hands. Trying to show my sympathy by my actions, I delicately placed the pan and gauze pads on the table beside Paul, avoiding a direct look at him, and by then Brother Felix sat beside him and began gently swabbing his face.

"I'm ashamed, Paul," he said.

Paul winced without moving his head. "You didn't do anything, Bro."

Brother Felix's eyes narrowed as he directed his gaze more intensely to what he was doing. "We all did it, Paul," he said; then he looked at me, and my skin went clammy. "Hand me a cotton stick, Casey, and the antiseptic there."

"Yes, Brother," I said.

He took them from me and continued to work. "When did the sores begin, Paul?" Brother Felix said.

Paul smirked. "How can you tell them from the other stuff?"

"They're very distinct," Brother Felix said.

"Well, what he said about the syph—I ain't got no screwing disease. I ain't touched nobody."

"I know that, Paul," Brother Felix said. He rose and went to the bookshelf and took out the medical encyclopedia.

While Brother Felix leafed through the pages, I was left alone with that look on Paul's face. I cinched the belt on my robe more tightly, then put my hand in my pocket. As soon as I felt the ammonia tubes, I withdrew it. Finally, Brother Felix began to read: "'A contagious skin disease characterized by blister-like pustules and yellowish crusts, often on the face. It is spread by direct contact with the moist discharges of the sores.'" He gazed away from the book, shaking his head sadly. "Poor Damian," it seemed that he said.

"What?" Paul said.

"No, no," Brother Felix said. "I'm sorry. It's called impetigo. It isn't serious, but by now almost every one of us has been exposed."

"I thought you said I had to be touched to give it to somebody else," Paul said. "Outside of you, there ain't been a soul—"

Brother Felix nodded agreement to what Paul must have just realized. "You went through that infernal paddling machine tonight, and before—"

"Yeah." Paul smiled. A strange light came into his eyes. "Yeah!" Then he laughed. "Well, I'll be d—"

The door opened quietly, and we all turned.

"Come in, Brother Luke," Brother Felix said.

He was followed by Brother Sebastian, Brother Francis, Brother Thomas, Brother Jerome, and Brother Gregory. As they came through the door, they took their hands out of their sleeves and removed their hoods, bowing their heads as they passed Paul, then standing at the walls and replacing their hands in their sleeves.

"The others will be along very soon," Brother Luke said.

"Casey, take Paul back to the dorm," Brother Felix said.

Paul stood up. "I don't need no help," he said.

"Here," Brother Felix said, "take these." He gave Paul a couple of pills. "They'll help the pain." Then he put his hand on Paul's shoulder and led him to the door.

After Paul left, he told me that I'd better go on back to my bed; but I moved into the corner beside the sink and showed him by my face that I was afraid, and he let me stay.

They all stood, silently waiting, until Brother Ignatius and Brother Anthony came.

Brother Luke spoke first. "He's in his office now. Brother John is watching from just outside the dormitory door."

Brother John was the shabby one who worked in the administration building.

"I am not so sure this is the way," Brother Sebastian said.

"Way?" Brother Thomas said. "We haven't found a way yet."

"I mean meeting like this," Brother Sebastian said. "Perhaps we should send a letter to the bishop and let him handle it."

"Signed by all?" Brother Luke said.

Brother Sebastian considered the question, then said, "If necessary."

Then Brother Felix spoke. "And what do we do in the meantime? It's out of hand now. The boys have more control than we do."

"Yes," said Brother Luke, "and we've let it get that way."

Brother Gregory, who worked in the fields, said, "What could we have done to prevent it?"

"We must pray," said Brother Francis.

"I'm sure we've all been doing that," Brother Felix said, coming to the sink and washing his hands. "Now we must take action, but it must be final."

"What do you mean by final?" Brother Gregory said.

"That it cannot fail," Brother Luke said. "Correct, Brother Felix?"

"Yes. Once we begin it, it has to end with Brother Lawrence's dismissal. There are places within the church that can take care of him peacefully. And he will continue to have all of our prayers." Then he told them about the sores and how they must be alert to send all the boys to the dispensary at the first sign of them. "And of course you must come yourselves, if necessary."

As I recalled his giving out the demos so unjustly after Mass that morning, Brother Luke pressed for the plan, and finally Brother Felix revealed it. At the Big Brothers Christmas banquet in two weeks, they were each to tell as many of the big brothers as they could about the cruelty of Brother Lawrence. They should be as factual as possible. Any brother who had witnessed a cruel act must not shirk his obligation to tell it. If it came to a hearing before the bishop—and it very well might—they must stand as one in their indictment. "The Big Brother Organization is composed of good men, compassionate men, for the most part," Brother Felix said. "We can trust them to do what is right. Tell them that you are firm in your conviction that such things as the paddling machine and beating up on boys in the dining hall and elsewhere, and in front of us, constitutes—"

"None of this may be necessary." It was Brother Jerome, a little gnome-like man who worked in the dairy and who, the boys said, loved cows more than people. He seldom spoke.

"Explain what you mean by that," Brother Luke said, emphatically, as if he needed to demand the information to get it at all.

Brother Jerome took his hands out of his sleeves and rubbed them together with sound. The tips of his fingernails were black. He licked at his mouth, as the blood rose to his coarse face. "Brother John came to the dairy today. He often does, just to get away for a while."

"Yes, go on," Brother Luke said.

"He said that there were two men at the office today." He stopped.

Brother Luke sighed. We all waited.

"He said he thinks they were there because of something to do with the Stanley boy." Brother Jerome seemed to have run out of words to continue, but he had run out of information. "That's all I know."

No one seemed inclined to question him further, except me, and I was so scared by then, I felt my nightly water trying to flow, and pinched it off with my legs.

"I have heard that," said Brother Thomas.

"Does anyone know anything more about the Stanley boy?" Brother Luke said.

"Only that he must have left with his sister," Brother Thomas said. "Nobody has seen him since her visit."

Brother Felix said, "Were they civil or criminal authorities?"

"I heard that they were civil," Brother Thomas said.

"I believe criminal," said Brother Jerome. "But only Brother Lawrence spoke with them, in his office."

"I would like to avoid anything…legal if we can," said Brother Felix, "but we'll just have to wait. What has happened to Paul is plenty enough for Church action." And he added that they must all be willing to speak out, though secretly of course, "when the Big Brothers come to St. Francis for the banquet. Let us pray."

The brothers knelt and I knelt with them, though the movement caused a trickle until I could pinch it again. Brother Felix spoke some touching words about love and brotherhood, and then they left. I was to clean up and be back in my room in five minutes.

As soon as they were gone, I went to the criggy across the hall, leaking a little. Then I went back to the dispensary and put things away and wiped it all clean. My hand brushed the ammonia tubes in my pocket, and I returned them to the jar. Then I scrubbed my hands with the liquid hygienic soap and rinsed them with water hot as I could stand it.

After I had locked the door and was on my way to the stairs, I remembered that I had left the little shoes behind. By then, I was too tired to go back for them.

Mt. St. Francis School

November 25, 1947

Dear Mother,

Just a few lines to let you know I got my winter coat but I forgot to let you know. I've been pretty busy here. It sure comes in handy. It gets pretty cold sometimes. But it isn't too cold.

For Thanksgiving we had fruit cocktail, turkey drumsticks, mash potatoes, and peas. Then some of the boys put on a funny play. Then we had a cup of ice cream and cookies. We really eat o.k. here.

Vinny ask me to send you his grades for October and here they are. Religion C, Reading A, English B Spelling B, Arithmetic C, Geography C, History B, Penmanship C. You already got mine a long time back.

Well I'll be closing for now.

With love,

Casey (and Vinny)

P.S. We got the two dollars but they are running out.

It was hard to write letters anymore, because I was spending so much of my time writing one kind of note and making another kind for a plan I had thought of to help Brother Felix's along. I figured that if I wrote three a day of the first, I'd have 39 by banquet time; if I made one a day of the others, I'd have 13.

I was busy too because so many boys came to the dispensary to get their sores treated. Lawrence had quit coaching the midget basketball team, and when Brother Luke took over one of the first things he did was to replace me at guard. I stayed on the team a day, and then quit. I told him I had to work with Brother Felix a lot and that I wasn't much interested in playing basketball (I almost said pussyball) anymore.

I thought Paul would disappear like Blue and Carroll, but he was still here, pining in his bed whenever he could, hanging around the courtyard; he seemed to be waiting for the day when everything would come to a head. It was Lawrence who had almost disappeared. He didn't come to the dispensary like the others, or even to the dining hall, but those who saw him from time to time said he had sores on his face like so many of the rest of us. I had them, too.

But Vince and Moon didn't; they must not have hit Paul when he went through the machine. Maybe they'd been peeling potatoes that night. But I could not claim a perverse brotherhood with every boy with sores on his face. Several had them who had not been there—the fly boy, for one. He'd been sick in bed. So the ones who had the sores had either hit Paul or caught them from somebody who had, or maybe hadn't; the ones who didn't have the sores had either not hit Paul, or the sores hadn't taken. There was no way of knowing, except for what I remembered of that night. In the end, I knew with certainty only that three who had hit Paul had the sores: Lawrence, Kurt, and me.

A week passed, and I was on schedule with the notes. It was a tedious job finding the right words and letters in pages torn from rec-room magazines and school books then cutting them out with the little scalpel I borrowed from the dispensary. I searched hard for full words like *and, do, with, things*; I even found an Elgin wristwatch ad. My bed-wetting had all but stopped that week, mainly because I spent a good part of each night in a criggy stall working on that batch. The other ones I wrote during the day, in class. I kept them all in my locker, in various pockets.

On the First Sunday in Advent, six days before the banquet, I was scheduled with Abel Zablonsky to serve High Mass. The evening before, I had at last made a good and full confession. I told the Father about my role in Blue's and Paul's beatings, what I had seen Kurt and his buddies do to Carroll's sister, Lawrence looking through the keyhole and what had happened in the room, and all of my pitiful, fake attempts to confess. By the time I admitted that I had taken Communion several times, knowing that I had mortal sins on my soul, Father said I was being too hard on myself; he assured me that I was now free of it all, returned to the state of grace. When I asked him if I should tell what I knew, he said that I would do the right thing when the time came, he was sure. Then he told me to say a rosary, "Not because you have sinned so heavily, but for Brother Lawrence and the others, and for the souls in Purgatory."

"Yes, Father," I said.

"Now say a perfect Act of Contrition, my son," he said.

And it was perfect, or as nearly so as I could make it. When he told me to "Go in peace, and pray for me, my son," I answered, "Thank you, my father." But it sounded all right. After rosary that night I lay in my good pajamas, on the unsoiled side of the mattress, and slept through until dawn.

I woke clean, luxuriant with having been so thoroughly forgiven, transformed as I looked at the wooden ceiling and painted walls on which hung a gallery of pictures of saints, each with a halo. As I fixed on The Little Flower, recalling the story Brother Felix had read to me about her, my spirit seemed out of my body, off in some place like the city Brother Felix had told me so much about. For I was more than forgiven; I was chastened, trembling with the idea of the delicacy of what I had regained, what had been so easy to lose.

In the sacristy that Sunday morning, when Abel and I returned from lighting the altar candles and Father Larson (Father Shorty's real name) was donning his sacred vestments, we stood head to head, anticipating the miracle we were about to perform. I watched with folded hands as he vested, lifting the waist of the Alb and tying it with the Cincture. He could do nothing much with the sleeves but keep raising his arms from time to time to let them fall up. Lucky for me, we shared the shame of being small, for he always helped me with my cassock and surplice in the same way.

Everybody rose as we walked out, and I was proud to be leading our little trio of holy musketeers, armed with only a book and a chalice. I was singing inwardly with the brothers' Gregorian chanting from the front pews. The Latin cadences flowed into the dark crevices of my remainderd guilt, washing them clean; the mixed aroma of candles and altar linen and flowers was like hyssop (what I'd heard about it) to my nose. I thought I knew now something more about why what I was a part of was called a sacrifice.

After *The Prayer* and just before *The Epistle,* Abel and I walked with the priest to the Sedilia at the side of the altar; held the back of his chasuble and, as he sat, draped it over the bench; then took our seats beside him. I was on the inside, nearer the sacristy door; and as I fidgeted down to comfort, hearing the boys' choir opening of *O Come, O Come, Emannuel,* I had an eerie feeling that I was being watched. I tried to look around without moving my head, but I was so far from anyone but the priest that I finally glanced at him. His face was in complete repose, and I moved as if to settle myself, taking the occasion to sneak a look at the sacristy door. It was shut, and so I folded my hands on my lap and looked at them. "That mourns in lonely e-exile here...." The choir had the tinny sound of boys singing soprano.

Slowly I raised my head. When I saw the feet, I knew. They were held together on the sloping block near the bottom of the cross by a spike, the head of which seemed a protuberance on the upper foot. I let my eyes go up, over the knobby knees, the loin cloth, the punctured side, to the head fallen onto the shoulder. The eyes above the hollow cheeks, beneath the thorns, were in direct line with my own, and should have been closed; but they seemed from my view to be open just enough to see, way down here, the only thing they could: me. By then the choir had finished and the priest rose for *The Epistle, The Gospel*, and The Homily; and I could look at him, at the congregation, and, quickly, at Abel.

At Communion, hearing the opening of *Panis Angelicus*, I held the Paten for myself then let the Host dissolve slowly on my tongue, as I rose and followed the priest. First to Abel, who remained kneeling on his pad on the altar step; then to the Communion rail and the brothers, most of whose faces were clear of the sores; and to the boys. Theirs, mostly, had receded to faint scabs. A high, clear voice, like a girl's, sang throughout; and I tried in vain to see whose it was. The sound of the words made it seem as if the angels had indeed carried the wafers from heaven. To avoid having my teeth touch the Host, I kept my mouth perfectly still. As I placed the Paten beneath the various chins, scrutinizing the faces, I needed to swallow; but I would not let myself, and by the time I handed the Paten to the priest at the altar table, my mouth was awash. Still I refused to swallow, handing him the wine cruet, Abel handing the water. We returned to the steps, and then I let it all go down, realizing that Lawrence had not been at the rail.

We walked around the courtyard in our white shirts and neckties and jackets, biding time until the noon meal. I was aglow with that post-Mass feeling, *Holy God, We Praise Thy Name* still ringing in my head, the feel of the priest's hands in blessing still lightly on my head, when Vince came up. I was as surprised that he was seeking me out as I was that he was without Moon.

"Hi, Vinny," I said.

He wanted to know if I had received a letter yesterday, with money in it, and when I told him I had he asked for his dollar. I gave it to him; and he put it in his pocket, straightened my necktie, and told me we would be back home in a week.

"Are you off the blacklist?" I felt elevated but tried to sound humble. I had said on my knees, over and over, *"Lord, I am not worthy that Thou shouldst enter under my roof..."* and the rest of it. It was good for five years each time, and, hoping that indulgences could substitute for demos, I'd been transferring half of all I'd accumulated since we'd been at St. Francis to Vince. Maybe it was working.

He smiled. "It won't make any difference. You'll see." Then he punched me playfully on the arm, in the old way, and said, "I suppose you have enough merits to wipe out the whole blacklist."

I laughed. "Not hardly," I said. Holiness felt good, but Vinny was acting like a buddy again!

"Kurt's got about 500 demos, and I guess his two sidekicks got more than that," Vince said. "They get caught all the time."

"He's going to get more than demos," I said.

"What you mean?"

A voice inside me said, You'll see. I said, "Ah, I don't know."

As I spied Rollo, strolling like a plump guard at the edge of the crowd, it came to me that I had not made such a perfect confession after all. How about my pitiful attempt to bully him? But then, he'd got the upper hand fast enough, along with the candy—he'd almost taken a chunk out of me—so I figured it was even. Besides, having honestly forgotten, I'd said, as I always did anyway, the handy little catch-all: *I am sorry for these and any other sins I may have committed.*

When Vince turned to go, I mingled in with a nearby group. There was a new boy among them, dressed rather elegantly in a knickerbocker suit and necktie; long, white socks; and shoes with buckles. His hair was sandy, and the corners of his mouth turned up in a permanent smile, so that little wrinkles formed at the sides of his nose. He was elfin cute, littler than I was; it was as if Little Lord Fauntleroy had stepped out of the book, and been sent immediately to Mount St. Francis.

Some of the boys were razzing him, but he just stood his ground, letting the smile work. And then he spoke, in a voice like a young girl's, and I realized that he was as scared as I had been on my first day, that the smile was covering up the fear.

"I'm nine," he said.

So I had been replaced as the youngest. Instead of disappointment, though, I felt I'd risen a notch.

Several in the group turned to me, wagging their heads.

I held out my hand to the new boy, and we shook. "What's your name?" I said.

"Edward Everett Norton." He said it as if it should not ever be broken up. I wondered why somebody like him had been sent to this place, or if, like Vince and me, he was there but didn't have to be. (Was that what Vince had meant when he said, "It won't make any difference. You'll see"?)

Suddenly Elgin said from the pulpit, "Oil the machine for the new kid."

I had not seen Kurt or his buddies in several days, had in fact almost forgotten about them since the meeting of the brothers in the dispensary. But Elgin must have been at Mass, for he wore a necktie and a jacket, so small on him it seemed ready to split up the back.

Several boys began to form, others walked away quickly into the dorm, and some of us stood by, looking around. It wasn't done in full daylight, and not when we were dressed up.

Elgin looked at Edward Everett Norton. "Little Norton here will be ten on—get this—Christmas Day." Then he came down and began to push boys into line, taking Edward to the front with him. "Okay, J. C.," he told Edward, "get down on your knees. This is your initiation—"

But Brother Luke and Brother Sebastian came, swinging their ropes. "There will be no more of this," Brother Luke said. "Now, get on to the dining hall."

Mt. St. Francis School

December 3, 1947

Dear Mother,

When you get this it will be my last letter before we're home for Christmas. But we still don't know how we are going to get there.

Next Saturday is the big banquet. They say the Big Brothers give presents and some girls from Madonna Vista come over here. Maybe Cousin Janet Faye will come with them.

Well I can't write too much right now and so I'll be closing.

With love,

Casey and Vinny

Friday evening, the day before the banquet, I tallied the notes. A little short of my goal, I had hand-printed 29 of them.

Write a note to a Big Brother. Say what you don't like about this place. Tell something that really happened. Put the note in an overcoat pocket in the cloakroom at the banquet. Write more than one if you want to.

That night I placed them inside the shoes of 29 selected lockers.

I had completed 11 of the other notes of patchwork words and letters pasted onto half pieces of paper. They were not so readable, but they'd do. I wanted to make two more, but since I could not distribute the other 29 all at once, I had to stay awake in bed waiting for the right time and couldn't work in the criggy. I made sure Paul got one, and Rollo, and the fly boy. Mickey Rickey, too. And even Edward Everett Norton, who, I now knew, had sung *Panis Angelicus* last Sunday. I only wished that Blue and Carroll could write one, and I thought briefly of doing it for them, but I'd run out of time.

The next morning I was careful not to look at anyone at his locker. Even a glance could betray me. So during voluntary Mass and Saturday morning classes, I pretended extreme occupation, first at my missal, then at my school books which—heaven help me if a brother saw them—I had cut to ribbons with the little scalpel I had borrowed from the dispensary. But occasionally I did look around during classes, hopeful that all or most of the 29 were composing their own secret charges.

The banquet was to coincide with the evening meal. I dressed early so that I would not be at my locker when the others would be so loudly near. During the next hour I idled at the pulpit for a few minutes; had the run of the rec room, where I shot some solitary pool and played a game of pinball; then, basking in solitude and the lax rules on such a special day, decided to go to Queenie's pasture to say good-bye.

I didn't hear a sound as I walked along the fence and approached the rise of the slight hill below which she usually foraged. But there she was, and when I went around to her she looked only with her eyes as she snorted visible breath. Her head remained down. I searched for candy, finding only the eleven notes in my jacket pocket, and a dollar bill.

I looked around, to make sure I was alone, because I knew I was close to saying something meant only for her. But I wasn't so sad; I wasn't even cold. I was in the state of grace, I was dressed for a banquet, and in two days I was going home to the mountains. I wished she was going with me. *We'd go riding in on Main Street. I'd be astride her honey-colored back in a squeaking leather saddle, holding a silver bridle and shaking out music as we went. And somewhere, maybe right in the middle of the crowd, she'd rear and whinny like nothing they'd ever seen—*

I saw a movement across the way. It was only Brother Jerome, thick in his robe, leading a cow. From such a distance he and the cow looked like a painting of some old scene from one of Brother Felix's picture books, and I thought again of the city I was named after and saw in my head a grove of crooked trees and a winding river with a bridge, all bathed in a special light, like the glow around saints' heads when they walked the earth. Then I wondered what Brother Jerome had meant when he had said that "None of this may be necessary." I took out one of the notes.

BROthEr LAwrEnce waTCHeD KuRt and elGIN and
MOOsE dO imPuRe tHInGs with cARrOlL's SiSTer.
i sAw HiM.

Something was not right about it, and now I knew what it was: they wouldn't know who i was unless I signed it. Which of course was why I had spent a good part of the last thirteen days cutting and pasting letters in the first place. But that little i was pitiful; only a coward would think of it. The priest had said that I had been too hard on myself, that I would do the right thing when the time came. But bearing traceable witness was not high on my list of choices. I tore off the last line of all the notes and wadded up the little pieces of paper into a ball. I reached through the fence. She took it from my hand like an apple, and I patted her jaw and said good-bye.

For the noon meal we had eaten bag lunches in the rec hall and gym; only the ones on the blacklist—those working on the decorations—had been allowed to miss classes. When I walked into the dining hall, among several other boys, I glanced in at the cloakroom to see a few men's overcoats. We had been told to leave our caps and outer coats in our lockers. I turned back, feeling like a gentleman, until I saw Vince and Moon and Paul and the others, in white jackets, standing around the walls. "It won't make any difference," he'd said. And it didn't seem to, to him, as he smiled and talked to Moon and even Paul. The festive occasion seemed to have relaxed even the blacklisters.

The place had been transformed since breakfast. The tables were rearranged in three long sides of a rectangle. A large Christmas tree stood near the back wall, its blue lights shining coolly. Near-life-size figures of the manger scene circled the tree, and in front of that was the central table. It was all symmetry, an opening up of the former rows of crowded tables so affecting I wondered why it could not have been so all year.

We were to find our assigned seats, marked with a place card, ten-year-olds at the far right. As I searched mine out, several men entered laughing. The card to my left said Dr. Franklin O'Brien; the one to my right said Jeremy Stitch. We were to stand behind our seats until everyone was there, and I did so, looking down to see a wrapped present beside my plate. I was almost in direct line with the center table, with a good view of the men and boys coming in. The kitchen door was near the end of the table to my right, some ten seats away. Between every two boys stood a Big Brother, more than I had planned on. I hoped eleven of them had worn overcoats.

When Dr. Franklin O'Brien came to his place between me and Mickey Rickey, he introduced himself to each of us and read our names from our cards and shook our hands. As he began talking to Mickey, I looked to my right. Still no Jeremy Stitch, and I asked Abel next to the empty seat who he was. Abel pantomimed catching a fly and gobbling it; and even though the flies had disappeared, I was grateful not to have to contend with him this night. Until I wondered where he could be.

The central table was by then almost filled, with most of the brothers in their brown robes, several men in dark suits, and Father Larson. A big priest, dressed like Father Larson in black suit and Roman collar, walked around the far wall and stood at the center of the central table. Across the long side of the room from the big priest, in the center of the longest table, stood Edward Everett Norton between two big Big Brothers.

Doctor O'Brien turned to me. "How have you been getting along at Mount St. Francis, Cosimo?"

"Okay," I said. "But call me Casey, sir."

He looked puzzled. "Irish?" he said.

I gave a little laugh. "No, just short for…what's on the card."

That was all for now, because the big priest raised his arms and the room became quiet. We all joined him in the everyday prayer, and when it was over he spoke, in the voice of Brother Lawrence.

He *was* Lawrence.

He introduced the Big Brothers at the head table, then seemed to be talking to them as he gave a little speech about Mount St. Francis. He recounted the history of the school, when it was founded and why, invoking several times the name of its patron saint and, once, the saying on the crooked plaque on the stone pulpit. He welcomed everybody, expansively, as if nothing was wrong; and then he let Father Shorty bless us all.

Lawrence remained standing as the rest of us sat, and then he introduced Edward Everett Norton. "I believe he's going to sing for us now," Lawrence said; then he nodded to Brother Francis and sat down.

Brother Francis reached under the head table where he sat and took out a guitar. As he walked around the table to the center of the room, Edward joined him there, and he played while Edward sang in his high voice a ballad in Latin I had never heard. When he sang the word *Christus*, he rolled the r; and when he sang *natus est*, he drew out the u so hauntingly I felt an unearthly pall descend over the audience. I looked for Lawrence, seeing on the left side of his face what seemed like half a frown.

And then the banquet began. The servers brought out plates already apportioned: half a small chicken (or bird of some kind), mashed potatoes, and peas. Covered baskets of fresh rolls had been placed around the table, and soon we were all busy with the food. But where were the girls?

It had just occurred to me, when Doctor O'Brien turned and said, "What would you like to be when you grow up?"

I swallowed down a gob of potatoes, thinking, *Why did they always ask that?* "A doctor," I said.

Doctor O'Brien was so close to me that when I faced him I could count the whiskers peeking out of his large chin. He wiped his mouth with his napkin and made a little sucking sound to get the food out of his teeth, then said, "Oh? That's fine."

"Is it hard?" I said.

"Being a doctor?" he said.

I looked at his place card, and he followed my eyes. "Oh, I'm not a medical doctor. I'm a doctor of education."

I started to say that I didn't know pupils were sick, and then I considered Jeremy Stitch.

"It's just a title," he said. "I'm a high-school principal."

So I was sitting next to another headmaster. But he was a nice one.

Vince was passing behind us with a tray, and he stopped and bent to me on my right side, by the empty chair. "It's working," he whispered.

"What?" I whispered back, without knowing why.

He wrinkled his brow, as if I should know. "The notes," he said through his teeth.

"What—"

"Come on," he said, scoffingly. "You're the only one who would think of it." He motioned with his head. "Look." As some boys were getting up, others were returning to their seats. "You ever see so many guys have to go to the criggy before?" Then he winked and went on with his tray into the kitchen.

"Open your present," Doctor O'Brien said, kindly.

As Abel got up and walked behind us, I took the colorfully wrapped box by my plate and looked at it.

"It's just a little something," he said.

I moved the green ribbon aside and pulled it off, then carefully unwrapped the red paper. Within the box was a matched Sheaffer fountain pen and mechanical pencil. I'd wanted such a set since I first learned how to write. But now that I had one, I felt shamed that I had received it from a stranger, and I knew what the look had meant on the faces of mountain boys back home when Vince and I had gone with the priest to take them food and toys at Christmastime. I put the top on the box and set it back by my plate. "Thank you," I said, but I didn't look at him.

Then I did, as he put his hand lightly on my shoulder and said, "Please accept it in the spirit in which I have given it. It isn't charity, my boy. When you're a doctor, I'd like to think that you will use it to write out your prescriptions. Why, I'd be helping the sick."

When I put the box in my jacket pocket, I felt the notes. Abel had returned to his seat. "Thank you," I said, smiling at Doctor O'Brien, who wasn't a doctor. "I have to go to the bathroom."

I hugged the wall all the way, feeling occasional glances, and when I reached the vestibule there was a boy in the cloakroom. He didn't see me, and I turned quickly and went into the bathroom. No one was there, and I stood behind the door for a while, then opened it and went to the cloakroom.

Glorious overcoats! They hung in profusion, covering all the hooks. Extras were piled on a table. There must have been every name associated with cloth that I had ever heard: tweed, twill, camel's hair, hound's-tooth, cashmere. What great, good luck that the Big Brothers had come in winter.

I quickly planted the eleven notes, sampling for the others as I went. Vince was right: boy, was it working.

Feeling a presence, I looked at the doorway. It was Vinny! He'd been watching me, and now he smiled and said something. As I reached the door, I saw that Moon was with him.

"What are you two guys doing?" I said. "You want to give it away?"

"Nah," Vince said. "We just been waiting for you to—"

"Let's go to the bathroom." I led the way.

Moon was serious, silent, whenever I was with them; but when I watched from a distance, he usually seemed to be talking as much as Vince. I felt that he was always just waiting for me to leave. Inside the bathroom, he turned sullen. "Let's get out of here," he said to Vince.

"You mean now?" Vince said.

"No," Moon shot back. He looked disgusted that Vince could have misunderstood him. "Let's just go back to the kitchen."

"Go ahead," Vince said. "I'll be back in a minute."

When Moon was gone, I asked Vince what he had meant.

"I wasn't going to tell you," he said, "but we're breaking out."

"Running away?" I said. "Why? We go home tomorrow."

"*You* go home tomorrow," he said. "I don't know if I go anyplace or not."

"Why not wait and see?" I said.

"'Cause then it might be too late," he said.

"Don't do it," I said. "They can't keep you here."

"Well, how you going?" he said, with sarcastic finality.

"Don't know yet," I said. "They'll send somebody, or something."

"How you know?" he said.

I was mad. "She said so in the letter."

Now he was mad. "Well, I ain't taking any chances. If your name's in red on the chart, it says in big letters CAN'T GO HOME FOR CHRISTMAS. Clear enough?" He started for the door.

"Don't do it," I said, wondering why it wasn't called the redlist. He stopped and heaved his shoulders in a sigh of impatience, and I said the first thing that came to me: "When you going?"

He smiled wryly. "Why? Don't tell me you want to come along. You couldn't get on the blacklist if you tried to."

"But when?" I said.

"If I don't tell you, you won't know," he said.

"How you going?" I said.

He threw up his fist and jutted his thumb, jabbing it back and forth. Then opening the door, he said, "That was some plan you put together, Case"; tossed off a jaunty salute; and added, "See you home, Saint Cosimo."

➤ ➤ ➤

There would be no group rosary that last night. Boys who had parents picking them up left after the banquet. The blacklisters stayed late at the dining hall to clean up and would be required to attend regular nine-o'clock Sunday Mass. The rest of us were free to get ready to leave tomorrow and go to bed early, especially if we would be attending seven-o'clock. It all depended on when we were leaving, as it was announced by Brother Felix at the end of the banquet, before we said good-bye to the Big Brothers. I had left the dining hall just as soon as I could, while the church brothers were talking to the Big Brothers and they were all moving toward the cloakroom. I went straight to the dormitory, took off my jacket and necktie at my locker, and went to my bed, where I removed only my shoes, then got in and covered up my head. I must have gone to sleep immediately.

I had not thought of silent rosary, or the towel for early Mass, or the pajamas, or any of the other business. I wanted only complete and utter solitude. I wanted to get through the night quickly, unconsciously, then wake up and go home, for good.

"Where did they go?" Someone was shaking me awake. I tried to pull the covers back over my head, but the hand was stronger than mine. "Where did they go?"

It was Lawrence.

I rubbed my eyes. "Who?" I said, but I knew.

He must have remembered what I had on him and thought that he could still keep me quiet, because his tone softened. "Your brother and Mullins have run away." He said it as if he were the heartbroken bearer of news that would shatter me. I couldn't see him too well, but the white collar let me know where he was. I was wearied beyond fear, so I turned away from him and jerked the covers up to my neck, holding on with all I had. He put his hand on my shoulder and whispered, "Go back to sleep. Your uncle's coming for you in the morning."

I heard him walk away, then stop a few beds down. Then Brother Felix: "Paul Jackson, too." Lawrence said something hateful, and Brother Felix said something in a soft whisper. Then Lawrence said something with "bed check" in it, and Brother Felix reminded him that taps was extended for the special night. Lawrence didn't like what Brother Felix said next and answered something with "pampered hoods" in it. They must have turned then, for what Lawrence said was clear. "They let some of the Shetlands out. Ran them down to the courtyard and—. Didn't you hear any of it?" But before Brother Felix could answer— or maybe he had, softly—Lawrence walked off.

I lay for an hour or so, trying to imagine the odd little horses in the courtyard, and wondering if Paul had taken Queenie again. Then when all was quiet and the light beneath Brother Felix's door was gone, I carried my shoes to my locker and got my mackinaw, then went down the back stairs and through the long corridor to the courtyard. Two pole lights shone in opposite corners of the quadrangle. I put on my shoes, hoping that Paul had taken Queenie, but resolving not to find out. Why had I not heard the Shetlands? It would have been some sight from the window, I thought, as I walked near the pulpit, looking for something they might have done. It must have been near dawn, for the dark was being pushed away, I could tell, as I ascended the steps of the pulpit. I felt as I had that day in church, that I was being watched, and I scoured the buildings for a light. Then I looked up. Just above the administration building, like a vast, illumined brow, the top of the moon brooded.

But I was as weary of my habit of making too much of things as I was of Big Brothers and church brothers and blood brothers. Only days before, I had yearned for real mountains, where only months before I had idled; now I longed for a city I had never seen, and for the storied, pictured places in books. Who was i? A schemer who laid up future graces or a true penitent? A secret or a truth? Was I Casey or a joke of a saint? In short, Goddamnit, was I a little flower, or a little prick? And now I just took the Lord's name in vain....

I bent to see the opening at the base of the pulpit. I had wanted to go in ever since I had first discovered it, and this was my last chance. As I descended the steps and went to my knees, the answer to my questions came. Having reaped the benefits of special status from the worst among them, I was their anonymous, cowardly informer. I crawled inside.

Within the stony, musty darkness I smelled the faint odor of human excrement as, standing slowly, I raised my arms. I could touch the middle of the sloping top with only my fingertips, lower down with my full hands. Something scraped my back, and I felt out the bolt ends I had forgotten must be there. I tried to turn one of the nuts, but it was hopeless. As I started to leave, I heard the sound of a door opening and closing. Then footsteps, and the sound of another door. I leaned my back under the bolts against the higher wall, slid down to a sitting position, folded my arms across my knees, and rested my head...

...you hear steps on the you crawl back through and stay inside both and you are out there and everywhere following him up to where he cancels mass nobody goes in that goddamn church yes brother where did those three four now cannot find the little flower either maybe we should let them all go where did he go and he rubs at whiskers only they are sores and he laughs him too when did he go the three big ones and more they have brought in circle him and drag him to the stone thing you are in looking through the holes and still out there too the silent ones in togas protest but make no move and some just go on to the church but it is closed so they kneel on the steps they pull him against the stone and lash him to it with his rope you are now just over his head at the holes and you are out there a part of the crowd too his arms stretched as far as they will go but his feet and the roly-poly one comes waddling through to take off his belt big as a whip and tie his ankles too the big one with a spear leaps from the top landing in front of him squatting like an ape hiya big fella and punches with a smile he can take it though wincing your turn big fella he says to the big one I give the word big fella they are going to cut your you got one the one always with the one you want to be with who has taken him off stands with one of those little carousel horses and lets it hose what is left of those bushes away let him try to cut that one off and laughs and all the time the tall good one in the toga pleads for gods sake dont do this the big one is now on top of the stone oil it up not that he cannot fit step right up and take a poke the one who stole the pretty horse has just been waiting for this and lets go with both fists and roly-poly is right behind with a bite they are lining up for their turn now and you are near the end on top everywhere the crazy one offers a bug says dopedopedope the tall sad one slaps then zooms back to his penny the homo prances by too good to stop what they are doing to him they are doing to you behind him you are so close he bleeds then stops and bleeds the ones in togas slapping a shoulder a tap with a rope a hand to the arm till the tall good one wipes his face with the hem of his dress boys are not hoods love is not pampering as the crowd is parting before your turn turning back to see her come weeping naked before him but only little jc is left curtseying in velvet want me to sing for you one of the big ones on top yelling hey where is the little prick his turn but the tall good one has untied him helps him to the church where they all wait they have just got to get in for breakfast but only he has the key he cannot find it tearing off the dress the black suit underneath then ripping off the church closed sign and lets them in singing cock-a-doodle-doooooo

I woke to voices. It was the chanting, but someone else too. Light showed in the rectangle, and I crawled out and went up to the platform of the pulpit. Brother John and Uncle Pasco stood on the steps of the administration building. Brother John turned back to the building, and Uncle Pasco started across the courtyard carrying two cloth bags, as the rooster let go again. When he was halfway there, I spoke with a wave. "Hello, Uncle Pasco."

"Hey, how you doing, kiddo?" he said.

I walked down the steps of the pulpit and went over and got hugged by him. "Where's Vince?" he said.

I asked him if Brother John hadn't told him about it.

"The one I was just talking to?" he said. "I had a tough time getting him to say anything."

So I explained it to him. When he heard the first of it—that Vince had run away—he started for the administration building, but I begged him off that. "He's gone," I said, "and I just want to go, too. I don't want them looking for him."

He said he saw my point, and that he'd hitchhiked half way across the country when he was Vince's age. "He's tough. He'll get there." Then he put his arm around me, and I led him up the back way to the dormitory. "Maybe we'll see him along the way," he said, as we passed the trophy room and the dispensary; and I asked him if they could do anything to him—make him come back to St. Francis—if they caught him first. He stopped. "Listen," he said, "they can't do a thing to him for breaking out of a joint he had no business being in in the first place." He squeezed my shoulder and shook me jokingly. "So don't you worry about it none. Your mother wants you both home for good anyway."

There were only a couple of boys I didn't know, and their relatives, in the dormitory. The suitcases we'd brought with us in September had been sent back home. Uncle Pasco opened one of the army bags, and we began to put my things in. When he reached in the locker to get the bad pajamas, I told him to just leave that pair and he looked a knowing smile at me and said, "Good thing. Say, you need to clean up a little, don't you? How'd you get so dirty on Sunday morning?"

I shrugged. "Just fooling around, waiting for you."

"So early?" he said.

"You're pretty early yourself," I said.

"Well," he said, "I thought I'd maybe get here in time to go to early Mass with you. Is there an eight o'clock?"

"Huh-uh. Seven and nine." I was afraid he might want to go now. It was just after seven. "I don't want to, here. Can't we stop along the way?"

"Sure," he said. Then he winked and added, "If we really have to. Now show me Vinny's locker and I'll pack it while you get cleaned up."

As I washed my hands and face, I realized that unlike the older boys I hadn't been at St. Francis long enough to get used to calling the bathroom a criggy. I had taken off my shirt and now saw that it was torn. I wrenched around to see my back in the looking glass. The bolt had raked me pretty well—or the bolts. There was a lesser wound near the deep one that stung but didn't bleed.

I changed my shirt and pants, we finished packing, and each of us picked up a bag and went through the aisles of beds to go down the front way. I wanted to stop by Brother Felix's room. As we passed my bed, I pointed it out to Uncle Pasco, then told him to go on down the stairs, I'd meet him in the courtyard. When he was gone, I stripped the covers from the mattress and flipped it over. There it was—the yellow spot—for all to see. But I didn't want everybody to see it; I wanted only Lawrence to. And now he probably never would. I tossed the covers onto the spot and went to look in Brother Felix's room.

He must have been at early Mass. If he wasn't, then maybe the trouble had started already. Maybe Lawrence had him in his office—. I made myself stop imagining what might be going on. I'd put the pen-and-pencil set in my mackinaw pocket, and now I took out the pencil and wrote on a pad on the small table in Brother Felix's little room.

Dear Brother Felix,

Thank you for letting me help you while I was here. I'll pray for you if you'll pray for me. Good-bye, Brother.

Your friend,

Casey Florentino

Uncle Pasco was standing by the pulpit. He hoisted his bag to his shoulder, and I tried to do the same, but it almost pulled me over. He helped me with it, and we carried the bags that way to the car.

I stopped when I saw it. It was a one-seater, bright yellow with white sidewall tires and dazzling chrome. Is it yours?" I said.

He smiled. "Mine and the bank's. I thought you might like it." He opened the passenger door, and I started to get in but wondered what to do with the bag. He took it from me and put both bags on the front seat. Then he closed the door and told me to come around the back with him, where he turned a knob and opened a RUMBLE SEAT! "Want to ride back here for a little way?" I sure did, I told him; and he hoisted me in, where I sat and sank slowly in the tan leather.

So I rode outside the car as we left Mount Saint Francis School for Boys, 1923, watching the buildings and then the fences and pastures become smaller and smaller. I wondered again at the name of a place that didn't have even a good hill, but the roll of the land was enough to keep me from seeing if Queenie was still there. As we moved through the farmland, there finally came a point where I had to stand to see the school at all; but a group of cows caught my eye, and I turned to look at them. When I turned back, Saint Francis was gone.

I slid down into the soft leather, a smell I loved, and put my arms out and propped my legs up. I rode that way awhile. A cold wind was blowing my hair, and I pulled up my coat collar and put my hands in my pockets. I'd wait that way as long as I could, but I knew that at any time all I had to do was tap on the window and my uncle would take me up with him.

The Error of the Rings

The Error of the Rings

"I might not tell everybody but I will tell you."
—Walt Whitman

MY SEVENTEENTH SPRING WAS NOT JUST A SERIES OF GIRL DILEMMAS, sports reveries, and acne battles; nor mere academic conquests, Good-Gulf blues, and girl glory. Not by a long shot. There was what I came to call, in my way back then of phrasing various episodes, The Error of the Rings. It was not an agony of the body, nor of the spirit, nor of the heart nor mind. It was a more practical problem, the kind that can get you into real, practical trouble.

In short, it was a financial matter.

As class treasurer, I had badgered my classmates with notices of overdue class-ring money until I became known (fondly, I assumed) as The Collector. I had no difficulty with most of them, since their fathers were "men with money" (as those of us without called them). I thought I had it all worked out down to the penny—tax, postage, the works.

But I had, for all my fastidiousness, made an indefensible mistake in pricing from the catalogue. I had overcharged everyone who had ordered anything fancier than the basic ring (who, again, were you-know-who). I discovered the mistake late, just before I was to send off the money for the total order. Now, I could have admitted to it, suffered the blow to my pride (for I had a sterling reputation in math), and re-calculated the entire order, refunding each and every overcharge. Or I could have (how shall I say it?) made adjustments.

I made adjustments.

Oh, how I adjusted!

There were only two who had not yet paid: Ezra Tyler, who lived not too far from me down by the coke ovens, and yours truly. I had been waiting to place my order last, but it was a relatively simple matter for me since I now had $75 in my savings account at First National, $9.57 in baby-food jars of change hidden in my room, three dimes in my un-turned-in Lenten card, five greenbacks under my mattress, and twelve bucks invested in the suit club at Cury's Dry Goods. I was flush.

But with the dilemma I needed a cause. The old injunction *lavorare est orare*—to work is to pray—came to mind; I'd overheard it from an atheist from the old country. But I didn't have time for doubting. I needed a penance! If I could pick up a couple hundred thousand years of indulgences along the way, so much the better.

Then I had it! I'd shuffle around some wealth.

Ezra had been sized when the ring company's representative had come around back in the fall, though I had not of course been pushing him for an order. I had in my sole possession all the money, all the documents—every shred of evidence. Supposed to build character, give The Treasurer on-the-job experience in the workings of commerce. And I must admit that it did turn out to be a lesson in financial wizardry. I came to learn that while I suffered pangs of guilt for years afterward, I might very well have been preparing for a position in business, or maybe government. I stayed late at Gulf City, where I worked, running my figures through the adding machine. I kept books now like a certified insane accountant. I found that keeping tabs under legitimate conditions is tricky, tedious, and exacting. But covering your tracks!—boy, that's a job for a genius.

I tabulated the OLD RING FIGURES and NEW RING FIGURES (what should have been) and entered them in my lockable diary, where my jumbled literary notes had to give way to the real world. And when I had it all worked out down to the final entry, there it was: $52.50, illegitimate revenue, on hand.

Well, you do what you can. I blew Ez to the deluxe job, and in a moment of monklike denial settled for the basic $18.75 version for myself. But even after I set aside $29.50 for his grand prix with delicious satisfaction—Ezra Tyler was going to have the equal of our richest classmates—I still had 23 dollars.

Yes, it was tempting to pay for my own ring with the balance. And I did consider it, I confess. But again, I compromised. After all, I had something coming for all my work, time, and trouble. This was no simple deal. Hell, I'd lost *weight*.

I kicked in $13.75 from my jars and other handy sources, pretty well cleaning out the stash in my room but without having to touch my bank savings. (Suit-club money was untouchable, thank God or Mister Cury.) Still, by the time the fiscal dust had settled, my personal ledgers were wrecked.

I know I'm pussy-footing on the subject. What it all came down to, was this: Five dollars of the extra 23 went to pay for my own ring. There's no other way to say it.

And still I had eighteen! How do you unload a surplus like that? Why, I'd worked a month at hard labor to clear that much. I had to justify that five, though. Earn it, so to speak.

I thought of giving the balance to Ezra outright, but I didn't want to make him an accomplice, not with real cash changing hands. And I wasn't about to risk exposure by turning it back in.

Maybe I could change its form.

It was getting near prom time, and Ezra, as far as I knew, had never been to anything. So I made up a budget for the things he would need—dinner jacket, bowtie, shirt, cummerbund, boutonniere, baby corsage for date (date?). Still, I had seven dollars.

So I bought a two-dollar Ingersoll at the five-and-dime and, passing the corner drugstore the next day, snuck the last of it, a fiver, into Ezra's dad's tin cup while he was playing banjo and harmonica against the wall, where he always was.

I defaced the diary with a knife, beat it beyond recognition with a crowbar, burned what remained, and buried the ashes on the hill behind main street under the oak tree next to Trixie. Then I took my last dollar from under the mattress, changed it to dimes at the Home Hardware, filled in ten more of the little pockets of my Lenten card, and finally rid my conscience of that obligation—though I still had to turn it in, no easy ruse in late May. (Why I hadn't thought to put the entire seven bucks in the card, I don't know. For the first time I could have filled in a large hole, even a rectangular slot. I guess I figured that if Father Flowers, by way of Holy Mother Church, was going to give it to the needy, I'd just saved him the trouble. Cut out the middle man, so to speak.)

On the late shift at Gulf City that night, I scrubbed the grease pit with kerosene and spent extra time cleaning the windshields and floormats and checking the hood of every car that drove in—anything to keep dolorous thoughts at bay. As I was tackling the rest room (I remember there being only one, for men), just before closing time, as always filled with loathing for the filth that, short of an armed guard stationed inside with instructions to shoot to kill, nothing could forestall, I mixed a paste of Bon Ami and water and with my little finger printed on the mirror:

WE AIM TO PLEASE.

YOU AIM, TOO. PLEASE!!

Then I washed my hands vigorously with Go-Jo. We'd been studying Macbeth in Miss McCrory's class all week.

❧ ❧ ❧

When the rings arrived, the beautiful new secretary had them sent up to me in Chief's senior homeroom, where we sat in his last-period history class, giddy with the approach of graduation day. Chief was in his relaxed mode, sitting on top of his desk, reading us a story, "The Doll's House," a welcome and, in my case, providential respite from the Peloponnesian and Punic Wars; and I simply put the box under his desk. By the time the story ended and the poor, tiny girl, named so poignantly "our Else," was sitting by the side of the road, nudging her older sister and saying, "'I seen the little lamp,'" there were eyes other than mine that were misty; and I felt assured of my beatific state. Then in that now doubly uneasy lull before the bell, Thurman Hatcher, Junior, whose father worked for the coal companies inspecting their own mines for safety violations, yelled out, as only he could, "Hey, I bet those are the class rings! Can we give them out, Mister Rembrant?"

I could have snatched that rich, addle-brained little twerp bald-headed.

Thirty-six of the thirty-nine graduating seniors in the class sang out in unison: "Yeah, Mister Rembrant. Please!" Our Else's plaintive words had been forgotten in the rush for gold.

What could I do? I had planned, before the error, to present each little box to its owner at the appropriate time, in reverse alphabetical order (in homage to Billy Wren and Denny Zay, who had spent the better part of 13 years unchallenged as last on every roll. Temporary relief had come to them half a dozen years ago, when a displaced boy from a Greek village joined our class for a while. He had an aloof, sullen, somehow statuary presence and dark, curly locks. It was as if one of those Hellenic marble charmers—a *kouros*, I think— had had it up to here with standing around in the raw and one day idled off his pedestal, headed straight to the sea where he scrubbed off a few centuries of guano, picked up some duds at the Athens General Store, had a reverse nose job, and come directly to Colton, Virginia, and The Barn, which is what we called our sixth-and-seventh-grade clapboard schoolhouse. There, even the teachers fell under his spell. Miss Gleam, our geography teacher, must have seen the Aegean reflected in his eyes; and our English teacher, Miss Wharton, with a rhapsodic sigh and surely a tip of the hat to Mister Browning, was heard to say, "Ah, I have looked upon Adonis, fair." What's in a name? Well, Aristotle Zusinides ((I truncated it to Zuse, and it stuck)) transcended poetics, religion, myth, philosophy, and the alphabet. He was the alpha and omega of 6A. I, being Latin and, by the way or, therefore, holding Donatello's *David*, which I'd seen a picture of in a book in Chief's apartment, in far higher esteem than any Grecian James Dean with a broken-off protuberance ((say, a finger, or worse)), thanked Jupiter that his counterpart's namesake—the girls called him Tottle and Zusy; I'll leave to the imagination what sixth-grade mountain boys, sons of coal miners and small-town merchants, came up with—that Aristotle Zuse returned to Mount Olympus ((talk about a mountaineer!)), where he belonged.)

Anyway, I had even begun writing a few ceremonial words for the occasion. But now, what if Ezra opened his box and everyone saw the deluxe? Worse, what if he blurted that he hadn't ordered one? And even if I managed to hide it, he'd have to sit there without one while all the others fondled and exclaimed over theirs.

In the confusion and pleading, as it seemed that Chief was about to give in to them, I reached in the alcove below his desk and whispered, "Back me, Chief. I'll explain later." To the class I said, opening the box from a crouch, "I'll have these ready to pass out in a minute. Uh, I think Mister Rembrant wants to tell you something first."

He rapped his big Pitt ring on the desk and said, "Turn to page 287."

There's no good way to describe the sound that followed, but everybody knows it. Call it The Groan.

Chief filibustered until the bell, and by then I had Ezra's ring and my own. Hunkered down like Quasimodo, I slipped Ezra's beneath my shirt and held it in my armpit. Then I emerged and, holding my own box in full view, placed the large box on the desk. "Here they are," I announced. "They're marked. Pick out your own."

Ezra and Bobby Jo-Jo Baird, the little eccentric who had boycotted ring-buying ahead of his time, went immediately out the door. The others fell on the box like a pack of jackals.

Chief motioned me aside. "What was *that* all about?"

I gave him my hurt look. "Can I tell you later, Chief? I promise it's something you'll approve of."

He let me go, and I caught up with Ezra walking against the wall, where he always walked. "Hey, Ez. Can I talk to you a minute?" I said it with no particular urgency.

As I let him into the boys' room and reached under my shirt, he perked instinctively. "It's okay, Ez." I gave him the box and stepped back, rubbing my hands on my dungarees, shifting my own ring box from hand to hand. "I didn't want to say anything back there, but a certain wealthy benefactress, who has requested to remain nameless, contributed the price of your ring."

He opened the box and looked.

"There is, however, one stipulation." Then I thought to drop the phony legal talk. This was Ezra Tyler, not Bobby Jo-Jo. "Ez, the lady who gave the money told me—or asked me—to ask you if you would mind keeping it, you know, under your hat till after we graduate? It probably sounds mighty strange, but she asked me if you would maybe just"—I speeded up—"well, sort of wear it on a chain or something around your neck till then?"

I had been avoiding his face. When I looked, tears spilled out of his eyes. Maybe we both would have been better off if I had just admitted my mistake and let them have their pound of flesh. I feared he might attack me for shaming him, or throw the ring in the commode.

But he was now gazing at the great beauty of burnished tin and a ruby-like stone with COLTON HIGH SCHOOL 1956 engraved around it. His face turned almost rapturous, and I knew then that I had done the right thing (at least as far as Ezra was concerned; I still could not rationalize fully my own profit on the deal). And then he laughed and wiped his nose on his shirt sleeve, and I felt that I had joined Tolkien, Browning, Wagner himself in that exalted station above all others—The Upper Ledge of the Ring Saga—whereat I was not just a fellow creator but above even that august trio, for I had achieved not mere paper or notes but the real thing. I had parlayed error into victory. Had turned *Götterdämmerung* on its ear, and was lifting off for godhood—

But there was Ezra Tyler, still earthbound before me in the boys' room, and so I said, passing vainglory notwithstanding, "Ah, what the hell, Ez? If you don't mind hiding it till after graduation, it'll be yours forever after."

"Thanks," he said.

"Oh, don't thank me," I said. "But I'll sure tell the lady who contributed the money that you'll, uh, honor her request? Okay, Ez?" I was desperate to exact from him, a promise, a grunt, anything.

"Aw 'ight," he said, finally.

"Oh, and, Ez? I almost forgot: She kicked in a little extra, for the prom. Now, she really didn't do *any* of this because she knows *you*—I mean, personally. I mean, she didn't identify you by name or anything like that. She just has more money than she knows what to do with, and she told me to use a little of her surplus for anybody who might want it. There's probably going to be at least one other guy who'll get some of her dough, too. You know how these rich dames are, huh, Ez?

"So, what the hell, Ez? Wanna go to the prom? What do you say?"

"Okay," he said, just like that.

"How about a...date? I mean, you have one?" God, I was making him feel like a leper.

"No." He was looking at the ring but, I could tell, thinking hard about what I was saying. I kind of shrugged. "Well, who—?"

"Maureen."

"Oh. Maureen." (Big Mo?) "*Great* personality."

"Yeah." He looked me in the eye. His lip quivered.

"You want to ask? Or you want me to?"

"You ast."

"Okay," I said. I put my hand on his shoulder, hating the gesture, but I needed to do something, for me if not for him. "Oh, I almost forgot, old buddy: I went ahead and ordered a dinner jacket and other stuff. Is a size 34 okay?"

He said it was, but I could tell that he had no idea about the size of clothes.

➤ ➤ ➤

In my ever-expanding territorial quest for girls, I had branched over into our sister coal counties in Kentucky. After several serpentine forays with Chief that winter—he was a top high-school basketball referee over there—I had snared a Harlan cheerleader for the prom.

Today, I had to go pick her up. But that afternoon was Chief's history exam. I told him a version of the story about Ez and the rings, using every Robin-Hood metaphor I could muster, then eclipsed the doctored-up tale of altruism with my more immediate logistical problem.

"Well," he said, but he hadn't fully fallen for it, "get back over here by four o'clock, and I'll give you the exam then."

Next to an offer to waive the exam, that's what I'd hoped he'd say. "Okay," I told him, and with great deference: "I'm leaving at noon, just after my trig exam. I'll be back in plenty of time."

"Take the car from the school lot," he said. "The keys will be in the usual place." Just as I was about to verify it, he added that when I took him home after the exam, I could just keep the car for the prom.

For casual subtlety, I chose to wear dungarees and white bucks and—a touch calculated to imbue my presence with Napoleonic flair—the latest addition in my growing collection of Sorrento shirts from Cury's: a powder purple short-sleeve with buttons the size of quarters on two sides of the front holding up a cloth panel. In a last-minute stroke of the rebel within me, with an embryonic vision of all the Big Bad Revolutionaries making their way at that very moment to Colton and all the other towns like it, I left a top corner undone.

I was worried, however, when I got behind a coal truck doing three miles an hour up Pine Mountain. But I made it all right and took Gracie, after a mostly silent hour and a half with her, to where she was staying with my friend Frances Freeman. While the girls went off upstairs, I sat talking plenty loud with Mrs. Freeman, so that Gracie might hear something of my full *academic* scholarship, books and stipend included. In the car I'd stolen only guarded glances at her. For her complexion was of that cherubic hue: whatever in a perfect blend would come out roseate, beige, coral. And her scent! I can describe it only with the sweet aroma of words: cardamom, rose hips, a light tinge of myrrh. To say that I was drunk on the aroma of her would be inadequate. I was anesthetized. I might as well have been a patient awaiting her scalpel as a suitor hopeful of favors.

But such beauty could blind, or tongue-tie, and I needed all my faculties. When I did look, she was fingering a large ring on a chain around her neck, an obvious reminder that she was still going steady with Tommy Ray Sutliff, the hotshot guard she'd all but had an epileptic seizure over on the nights of my trips to Harlan with Chief. So this was my last chance with her, I knew.

When I got to school, the janitor told me that Mister Rembrant had waited outside until the janitor's helper had given him a ride home! It was going on five o'clock. I had to pick up the dinner jackets and stuff; deliver Ezra's; take a bath and dress; shine my shoes; pick up Ezra and Maureen; pick up Gracie, Frances, and Pete. But I couldn't just go ahead and use Chief's car as if nothing had happened. He was probably too mad for me to go see him. So, I didn't have a car. I couldn't use Chief's, not now.

But that was nothing compared to the mess I had made of my scholastic standing. I went to the parking lot and started up the sleek, blue Studebaker Golden Hawk. The road into the mountains was calling. Oh, to feel the cool cover of High Knob, to know again the simple boyhood vagaries of Sand Cave and Flag Rock. But as I moved slow as that coal truck up Pine Mountain, I turned toward town, trying mentally to calculate what was left of my history grade. Why couldn't this have happened in English, or math, where I had cushions big enough to absorb such contingencies? I knew why: Asking Miss Collingsworth or Miss Allison to skip an exam to pick up a girl for a date would have been tantamount to requesting a license to murder her. Those two might have denied permission to "be excused" to someone with dysentery.

I pulled in to Gulf City, went to the adding machine, and ground out my fate: 69. It was like getting a D in Life.

I took a piece of paper from the boss's desk and, resisting various lines from Tennyson's *In Memoriam* and *Enoch Arden*, two of the seriously saddest poems I knew, made myself compose the simple words "I'm sorry" and signed it "Tonio," which only Chief called me.

I parked the car in the alley behind Chief's apartment over Earl's Restaurant; put the keys "in the usual place"; and, recalling that Miss Collingsworth had in the tenth grade called me "our Enoch," propped the note on the dash. It was 5:30; everything closed at six. At least I'd arranged to have Maureen's and Gracie's corsages delivered, big deal.

Idly I crossed the street to the swimming pool, went to the far side, and ascended the stone bathhouse. On Sunday evenings at Gulf City, then in my room at home, I often fell prey to moods of stupefying melancholy. I had names for various degrees of them: The Washroom Blues, No-Nox Nadir, The Vestibule to the House of Usher, and the like. But what I felt now was...it was as if, like a stray bug, I had wandered upon a thread and, questing after the beauty of silk, had found myself in a web.

It was that time of day in our town when something like a veil seemed to descend from the sky. It was as if the sun, gone over the mountains, had left a gauzy net behind; and as it began to settle, it changed everything below, putting glaze and shadow on the sidewalks and streets and a hazy glow over the swimming pool. Five-o'clock water was all different from noon's.

But there was no water yet. I was gazing into the pebbly concrete cavern of the empty swimming pool, recalling the times we boys had jumped naked in the moonlight from on top of the wall that enclosed the deck of the bathhouse, like the battlement of a small castle, where I had climbed and was now standing.

After a week of men and boys scouring the mountains with dogs, when Coach Carson and his battalion of grade-schoolers come to scrub and fill the swimming pool, they will discover me hunched fetally there in a corner. They will see on my wrist the cryptic scrawl in ink—futc—and take it as a clue; but only when they retrieve the wet scraps of paper from the lifeless form, will they begin to realize the full extent of my final agonies.

What will they find?

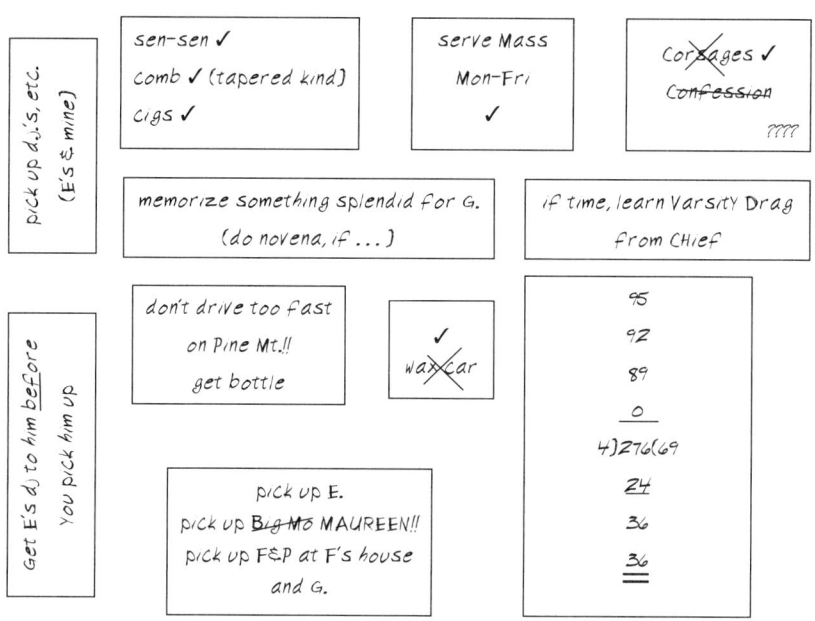

From out of all these scratchings, then, while a lovely daughter of the hills completes the Pietà by holding the broken body to her breast, the very bard I have fancied myself as some day becoming will emerge from among the grieving townsfolk and piece together my epitaph: He had a 92 going in to the final...and blew it!

I stood high on the wall, thinking of Lord Jim's "everlasting deep hole," the little lame prince, little Lord Fauntleroy. Metal clanged as coal cars coupled behind me, and I heard in my head's-ear the Anvil Chorus, the impress of the stamp of tragic legend.

But, wait. 69? That was a D+. Allowing for a little clemency, or an Error of the Grades, or a miracle, I could maybe eke out a 70. Which was a C-. Which would go down as a C. Which was average. Hell, I was average in my worst subject without even taking the exam! Maybe the new letter-grade system wasn't so bad after all.

Since I knew now that I would graduate—and I was already accepted at the University—a current transcript would be moot. Besides, with my nose in the books and my fanny glued to the chair, I'd redeem the C by making *A*'s there. Future achievement would surely outweigh past indiscretions.

As always back then, as soon as the problem of real substance was solved, the other ones, often merely logistical in nature, began falling into line, scrambling to let me know their solutions. It didn't make any difference what it was: clothes, money, car, job, sports.

In short, I had it!

I took off down the steps, across the side of the pool, made the wall in stride, then onto the path bordering what was left of old Tracy Field. I began dredging up "something splendid for G." Maybe a Shakespearean sonnet or, better yet, "How do I love thee? Let me count the ways." But it was too commonly used and, besides, an outright declaration. I couldn't propose. My mind went into Dyna-Flo, shifting selectively to the store of Miss McCrory's and Miss Collingsworth's memory work. "The Vision of Sir Launfal"? A good opening but, nah, I was using it for too many other occasions. "Thanatopsis" was out as well, though I'd maybe need it yet. "Tomorrow and tomorrow and tomorrow"? Huh-uh. Too lofty. Morbid, too. "The Barrel Organ"? I loved it, but I had already used it as a model for my upcoming toastmaster speech at the senior banquet. Besides, I needed something relatively fresh and, above all, splendid.

"The Highwayman"! Of course. Though on the sad side. Weren't so many of the good ones? If I could just get in a few minutes on it at home, I might be able to wing it, on a couple of stanzas anyway. The refrain took up a good chunk of it. I crossed to Gulf City.

"What you doing?" Zack said: "Goin' to the dance, or just gettin' in shape for it?"

I shook him off and flashed the phone a half dozen times for Bobbie Jean. "Get Uncle Vern for me, quick."

She said, "Do you know if Mother came by the station a little while ago to get gas?"

"No," I said.

"She didn't?"

"Don't know."

"You don't know if you know?" she said, as if I was deliberately retarded.

I sighed, loud, into the mouthpiece. "Listen, Robert—"

"You little snot," she said. "If I could get through this line, I'd slap your face for you."

I was at her mercy, and we both knew it. "I got to get a car fast, Bobbie Jean!" I whined, and Uncle Vern was on the line by then.

"Stiff date?" they said at the same time, then laughed and began talking to each other. She'd changed her tune pretty fast.

"Listen, folks, I'm kind of desperate here," I said. "You mind if we talk, Bobbie Jean?"

"Shoot it, kid," she said. "It's your nickel."

"Need the car?" Uncle Vern said.

"Sure do," I said. "It's prom night and I'm running late."

"Why didn't you just ask before?" he said.

I knew why. It wasn't because it was only a '47; I'd used it often. The truth was, I'd been locked onto Chief's new Studebaker. And not just because it was new. Because it was *Chief's*. "I thought I had other plans, till now," I said.

"I'll drop it off for you," he said. "Save you a trip up the hill. Keys'll be in the ashtray."

"Thanks," I said. "I'll Simoniz it tomorrow."

I was ready to tear out the door to the rental place, when the boss came in and said to Zack: "Better go on a little early, and give him a lift. Maybe save him from having a stroke."

"Let's go," Zack said. He got me to Appalachian Formal Rental, a partitioned section in Cury's Dry Goods, just in time; and when he dropped me at the house, I checked around the corner to find the hump-backed Hudson Hornet waiting. Black as a hearse. But it'd do.

All this by only minutes after six, and at 5:30 I'd been a sniveling suicide. I took the stairs two at a time, put the Ingersoll in Ezra's dinner-jacket pocket, grabbed the rest of his stuff, and took off for East Colton.

Returning home, I stood for a moment on main street, where we lived above my grandmother's currently empty store. It all looked so grand, as I thought of Ezra waiting for me outside his house, evidently to intercept me. His house could not have looked any worse on the inside than it did on the out-, only it was in- where the people lived.

Up I went, where, in the kitchen, my grandmother had pots of water boiling on the stove. To attract a renter, she'd had a water heater installed in the store and hooked up to the little room upstairs in the far back which contained, but barely, a tub and a commode. But it was too long a run, she proclaimed, and it was futile to try to convince her that it cost money to heat the stuff anywhere. She was concerned with the amount of cold water that had to run before the hot. It had to do with when she was a girl in Calabria, carrying water a long distance in a jug on her head. And it had a great deal to do with her brand of logic. A woman who'd come from the Old Country to Appalachia as a teenager alone, and with one eye, and who had then taught herself to read and write her native language from Italian Bibles didn't concern herself much with *arguing* a point. She simply *made* her point. She was a formidable foe, and a monumental ally. So I carried the water through the back hallway lined with olives and cheeses, peppers and bread; ran just enough cold to make it bearable; stretched out in the tub with my feet propped; and felt that delicious langor that always came with a night's promise of *girl*. I made a mouth out of my thumb crooked against the first joint of my forefinger, and began to practice on it. To get a reaction, I wagged my thumb, until I was smooching it. She wouldn't know what hit her.

Then I opened my eyes.

The room was painted over in peach enamel—walls, ceiling, linoleum. Even the tub which, since the enamel flaked on it, resembled a rub-a-dub-dub boat, overtaken by peach-tinted barnacles and dry-docked on claws. Although the inside bottom had pretty much returned to ceramic-and-black-iron. Looked like zebra hide. Mauzy and her bargains. And still had 25 gallons she'd bought at close-out—and with plans for the house, the furniture, the summer, and me.

I dried my hands and reached under the tub where I kept the yellowed anthology Uncle Ralph had left behind. I leafed through the thin pages and found "The Highwayman" and was just ready to brush up on it, when I sank too low too suddenly. The book was about as useful as flushed toilet paper, so I set the sodden mass on the stool and forgot about the black-haired Bess. It was too maudlin anyway, now that I thought about it. Maybe "Gather ye rosebuds while ye may...." But I had only limited time to create a literary sensation with Gracie and thereby save her from a humdrum life with Tommy Ray Sutliff. "...Now let us sport us while we may...." Ha! She had five grown brothers reared in Harlan, Kentucky. To spring the *carpe diem* on her would make me famous all right: *He changed the centuries-old, time-honored motif—from seize the day to seize the I-talian.*

It could all backfire. She'd maybe think I was too big for my—. I'd forgotten to order Ezra's britches!

Mentally transcribing *futc* from "fill up the car" into "failed utterly the Chief," I scrubbed the letters off my wrist, thankful that I had told Ez I would pick him up a little early, though just what I could do about the britches I didn't know. Everything was closed. Well, places could just be opened if need be. Mister Cury, a friendly man, would surely oblige. I had money invested there.

Moving around my grandmother's little jibes, I ate a spiced-ham sandwich on the run. At the small wash basin she'd finally had installed in the corner by the kitchen sink, I unscrewed Uncle Ralph's old double-edge razor and stropped the blade by running it back and forth across the heel of my hand to the rhythm of Eddie Fisher singing "Enn-eee-time, you're feelin' lonely..." on the television up front. Though I'd already shaved that week, I did it again, so the cologne would soak deep into my pores. This night, I needed not mere redolence, but saturation.

My grandmother sidled up, twinkling for a little combat. "*Perche* (why) you shavin' *demma due cappelli* (two hairs) for?" she said in her mixture of Calabresi, Church Latin, and Cumberland Mountain.

"Tell you the truth, Mauzy, I don't even have *two* today."

I brushed my teeth twice and sucked on a lemon. Then I doused my hair with Vitalis and combed it and went to my room, a partitioned half of the once-large kitchen, with that sense of well-being when fine clothes are laid out for donning. With my special cloth I dusted off "Serenade" from *The Student Prince*—my favorite song—and imagined while I shined my shoes and set my sock garters that I was going to pick up Ann Blyth for a Heidelberg ball. With a safety pin I affixed a rubber band to my boxer shorts and looped it over a bottom button of the starched shirt, all the time miming with Mario Lanza:

"From your window give me greeting. Hear my eternal vow."

I played the record again while with the shoe horn I oozed my feet into the shining shoes and tied the waxed laces with an extra knot. Holding with each hand the bottom of each trouser leg raised to the waist, I slipped each foot in, dropping each trouser bottom in turn and pushing each leg through just before the cloth could hit the floor. I zipped up, set the suspenders over my shoulders, finished dressing, and tilted the dresser mirror to see all of me I could. But it wasn't big enough, so I had to do it by sections: creases of the black trousers breaking just right onto the glistening shoes, cummerbund elegantly redundant, shoulders filling the white jacket. I steadied the looking-glass to reflect my head and torso and, adjusting the bowtie and gazing like Alice, saw after a while not Adonis at all but Miss Wharton, who, smiling, as if testing me, seemed to say:

Ah, I did once see Shelley plain.

Lifting my head, I gave back: "And did he stop and speak to you?"

Indeed, he did. And you?

"Better than he," I said. "'Twas Keats."

The spectral image of Miss Wharton smiled.

And now I prompted her: "'Where are the songs of Spring? Aye, where are they?'"

Think not of them, I had her say, thou hast thy music too—.

It was well worth the two-minute fantasy. I put my paperback *Golden Treasury* in my pocket and went into the kitchen.

Aunt Carm was there, come up to see "What's cookin'? I thought you was comin' home early for another facial—not that you need one, doll."

On special nights she'd give me a mud pack and squeeze anything vaguely resembling a blackhead. But this wasn't just special; this was it. My reputation, my future, my place in town lore might have been at stake. So we'd taken the precaution of having her give me the full treatment last night (good thing), and now she was here to see how the old kisser was holding up.

"I was lucky to make it at all," I said, rubbing my face to let her see its perfection.

She stepped back. "Myy-my," she cooed. "All gussied up!" But her face changed. She moved closer, her eyes scanning my face like radar.

She'd spotted something.

"Okay," I said, sighing extra loud, "what is it?" But I felt my face again and knew.

"Just a teensy-wheensy whitehead," she said, with that little smile of hers that meant: I don't care for me; if you want to go out lookin' like that, it's your business.

It wasn't just a "teensy-weensy whitehead." It was a stubborn white bb of pus that embedded itself near my mouth with the same regularity as The Curse, likely shot there by the same equivocating Hand.

"I'll have it out in a jiff'."

I couldn't imagine having missed anything the razor wouldn't chop off. It had picked the time between my shaving and dressing to make its perennial appearance; and if it wasn't taken care of right away, hours, maybe minutes from now, when I'd need every advantage, it could look like a grain of tapioca jutting out of my chin. Everything counted. So she went to work, and in a minute there was a small crater dangerously close to my lips. I took the lid off the rubbing-alcohol bottle; bent over and circled the pit with the mouth of the bottle; and raised up, my face to the ceiling, the bottle clamped upside-down over: The Blemish That Could Lose the Night. I flooded it for a full minute, then rubbed away the ring the bottle had made, slapped it several times, and said: "Grow back now, you white devil!"

I danced around with Aunt Carm, while she sang one of her old wartime favorites:

"IN A QUAINT CARAVAN, THERE'S A LADY
THEY CALL THE GYPSY...."

It must have triggered the witch doctor in Mauzy. "How's-a you warts?" she said.

"Gone to wart-heaven," I said. (She'd given me the burnt-broom-straw cure a couple of months ago.) But I shouldn't have used heaven. Her lips reacted immediately to the blasphemy. "Just kiddin', Ma," I said. "I never doubted you could do it. You said yourself unless I believed, it wouldn't go away. Well,"—I showed my finger—"see? Proof of my faith."

My kid sister gazed at my jacket, but she didn't think much of black flowers, fake ones at that, and she said so. When she touched the satin stripe on the trousers, I was again reminded that Ezra didn't have any and thought I'd better call him for his size. But he didn't have a phone; I wasn't sure if we did either, today. Mauzy kept one, on and off, by her little shrine to Mary on top of the television up front. But whenever we got too many calls, especially from girls after dusk, she'd have the phone taken out for a while.

She was too quiet now. I had to cut her in on the action. Ask her a favor or something. "How's about a little spell, Mauzy? Something that'll make me irresistible." I snapped my fingers jazzily. "How about the secret to the ol' Evil Eye?"

"Now, Tony," even Aunt Carm cautioned.

"Then I could cast my own spell on Gracie Lee. Come on, Maw. How's about the secret to the hex?"

Her lips had completely disappeared. You could get by with just about anything on a night like this, payday to boot, but you did have to be careful about the evil eye and other religious things.

"Aw, I'm only kidding, Mauzy Lee. But, come on, give me some power. I know: How's about telling my fortune?"

She was smiling now, and I settled my shoulders with a good move and a rustle. She took the cards from a kitchen drawer, and with half the deck in one hand she drove the other half between them several times. I reached up to touch my otherwise perfectly regimented crewcut, and saw in the mirror a few limp strands right where it counted most. As Mauzy began to spread the cards, reading them, her wrinkled lips making little popping sounds, her spectacles glinting like the eyes of a seer, I transferred some of her magic to the hairs, coaxing them to attention along with all the other obedient soldiers in the hirsutal battalion on my head. Studying the face cards, she stopped, backed up to pick up the meaning of a deuce, a tray. I was looking over her shoulder, Aunt Carm's arm around my waist. I knew that if she ran across the ace of spades before she found good luck she wouldn't let me drive tonight.

"This-a goorl, *Americana*," she oracled. "She's-a no fer you. She's-a give-a you hearts-a trouble."

"Awww, she's all right," I said, "for a Baptist."

She shook her head. "She's-a no fer you. You goin'-a marry pooty yellow-haired-a goorl. Pooty blue eyes."

Lord, what had I started? (How'd she know Gracie was a brunette?)

"Ma! (But!) Joosta minoots. '*Sta sera* (this evening) she's-a give-a you plendy good time."

"Now you're talkin', Mauzy Lee."

Aunt Carm came in on cue:

"Roll out the bar-rel. We'll have a barrel of fun."

"You *guarda* (watch out), chomp. Maybe she-s-a give-a you more than you want." It was as if she'd said, like the soothsayer she was, *Beware the double-ides of May.*

I saw the black ace peeking down the deck. "That's enough, Maw. All I wanted to hear." I had to get out of there, fast.

Careful not to mess my clothes, I hugged the women, gave my little sister a brotherly embrace and a dime, and made my way to the stairhead. There, on the wall, I brought Mauzy's two-way picture of Mary and Christ into alternate focus; when I had them merged, I started down the twenty-six steps, like Cagney. Halfway, where the stairwell began, I saw through the snow on the television below Mauzy's shrine by the window overlooking main street, a gyrating figure with a guitar, singing about a hound dog! Mauzy was heading for her chair, yelling like a bobby-soxer, "Ahh, my honey, my doll-a baby." She performed her act of excitement so well, she'd forgotten to tell me she would light a candle for me. But I knew she would.

⸭ ⸭ ⸭

At the corner cab stand—just big enough to house a telephone, a man, and a cigarette—I asked the perennial cab driver for a bottle of moonshine; and, as he went to the plain wooden shack around the corner, I crossed to the Hudson where, beneath a light jutting from the warehouse, I began searching *The Golden Treasury*, and came across "Young and Old" right away.

> WHEN ALL THE WORLD IS YOUNG, LAD,
>   AND ALL THE TREES ARE GREEN;
> AND EVERY GOOSE A SWAN, LAD,
>   AND EVERY LASS A QUEEN;
> THEN HEY FOR BOOT AND HORSE, LAD,
>   AND ROUND THE WORLD AWAY;
> YOUNG BLOOD MUST HAVE ITS COURSE, LAD,
>   AND EVERY DOG HIS DAY.

I especially loved poems with lad in them; this one had lass, as well. But then I read the other stanza.

> WHEN ALL THE WORLD IS OLD, LAD,
> AND ALL THE TREES ARE BROWN;
> AND ALL THE SPORT IS STALE, LAD,
> AND ALL THE WHEELS RUN DOWN;
> CREEP HOME AND TAKE YOUR PLACE THERE,
> THE SPENT AND MAIMED AMONG:
> GOD GRANT YOU FIND ONE FACE THERE,
> YOU LOVED WHEN ALL WAS YOUNG.

The old pull to melancholy rose up. But I couldn't have any of the old. I'd just use the first part and call it "Young." So with a mental apology to the author I ripped out the page and put it in my jacket pocket. I'd salt it away a line at a time.

The cab driver came over with a brown paper bag and handed it through the window. "Four dollars," he said.

"Four?" I said.

"'At ain't no Echo Springs," he said. "'At there's pure stuff."

I detached the paper clip from my wad of ten ones and peeled off four inner lessers.

He took the money with a laugh, then sobered. "Better watch that stuff. Hit can blind a man."

When he turned to go, I chucked the paper clip, folded the six ones into my pocket, hid the bag under the seat, and started up the Hudson, when one of our town's several winos—all harmless; a few, poetic—crawled out from under the warehouse. It was Gimme Rinelander, whose single request, to everybody, was: "Gimmethirtcentsumpmeat."

I had a nickel and a quarter waiting for him when he reached the window. As he bent to take the coins, he hit me with a blast of hali, which to this day has altered my olfactory system.

But then he doffed his hat, did a triple flourish with it, and bowed me onward.

Life was grand. Past mistakes would fade and wither with time. *"When all the world is young, lad...,"* my mind began.

At Ezra's house the smoke from the coke ovens was heavy, and he lived between two ridges so that full darkness came early there. He was waiting for me, again, though I had no idea what he had on for trousers. As he got in the car—the interior light, about the wattage of a lightning bug, was no help—I said immediately, "Ez, I don't know what I was thinking about, old buddy, but I forgot all about your britches."

"Oh, I had a pair," he said, casually and somewhat defensively.

"Well, listen, now," I said, "we can still—"

"It's okay," he said.

I didn't dare ask him about shoes.

I had a sinking feeling when Maureen, last in the back seat, wouldn't fit! They were so wired with crinolines back there, it just wouldn't work in a two-door car. But I couldn't be fazed: Gracie alone was wearing a knee-length formal, and what showed from knee to ankle was all woman.

I said, rather giddily, I suppose, "Maureen, will you ride up front, please? It's just that the three of you have on full dresses." (God, she was large. The cruel thought of going down to Gulf City for the pickup crossed my mind.)

So Ezra got into the front-middle, and Maureen took the passenger's seat. Pushing with both hands, I forced the door to a final click after her. Pete got into the back on my side with Gracie and Frances, and then I tried to get in. I was anything but broad in the hips, but there was room for but a single cheek of me. So I lifted up, slamming the door with my left hand, and settled my other cheek onto…the door handle. Which drove Ez into Maureen and me into Ez like their aslant podmate.

Giddy with the mixture of scents, I tried to take the helm, as I thought of it, since paradoxically the car looked like a hearse but now felt more like a life boat jammed with six desperate but hopeful youths. I could barely move. (At such a time one ought to be able simply to see beyond the immediate. Not I. I was agonizing over whether or not I was wearing my Saint Christopher medal!) I was driving and shifting across the wheel left-handed, my right arm as in a vise between me and Ez. What I wouldn't have given for a necking knob. And it occurred to me: What would we do after the prom? With Gracie up front with me, that would would mean one less dress back there; but getting four in the back, and one Maureen, would be like trying to re-install the middle Vienna Sausage.

"I can get Dad's Chrysler New Yorker after the dance," Peter said, with obviously similar thoughts on his mind.

"You couldn't get it now, could you?" It was Frances, and Gracie. As we moved along, though my mind was hurting with so much on it, one more image crowded in: Chief. He'd surely be where we were going.

Maureen's evening gown, billowed like a Genoa sail in full wind, obscured all vision to starboard. Since the ice would have to be broken between them some time, I asked Maureen if she would mind if Ez sort of held her dress down a little. Somehow she made room for him to scoot over, plopping my left buttock onto the seat at last; and, together, they luffed her sail and stuff, all the way to the Copper Kettle.

▸ ▸ ▸

I put the Hudson in crawl, negotiating the parking lot like a plump sea turtle paddling through the waters of sharks. At the merest turn I came dangerously close to large, shiny tail fins. I damn near wore myself out backing and pulling forward into a spot. You had to turn that wheel about four times around on each move. And my feet were doing double-time at the pedals. Now it was like driving a helicopter. Land, water, air—that Hudson covered the range of metaphors.

The others went on ahead, as I stalled with Gracie at the car. I asked her if she would mind if I put something in the box she'd brought her flats in.

"Whiskey?" she said.

I'd almost forgotten she was a Harlan girl. "Moonshine," I said, and a line from the all-but-mute role I'd played in *Pyramus and Thisbe* came to mind: *"Myself the man i' th' moon do seem to be."*

She asked for a little nip, right then and there, and I figured I had it *made*. And when into her lovely mouth she inserted a Wint-o-Green LifeSaver, and offered me one—well, let's just say that metaphors are destiny in the lives of the inspired.

Glenn Smith and The Cavaliers were playing "Sweet Georgia Brown" as we walked in and found our booth. Gracie slipped on her flats, and we hit the floor, doing two shags in a row. God, she was tough. I cuddled up to her on the slow ones and on the fast ones swung her around with such grace that I was certain the entire crowd was watching us and, better still, that she was already in love with me and my smoothness. I was sure that later, in the car, when I sprang "Young" on her it would be a mere coda to my suave start.

"*And every lass a queen....*"

As we separated at the end of a number, I cocked my head and gave her what I considered to be a wicked little grin, something only the two of us would understand, that magic that exists between the greats: Fred and Ginger, Gene and Cyd, Marge and Gower. She was a package of pulchritude and haloed with the flora of immortal poetry: the rhodora; a red, red rose rose rose; the entire host of daffodils. As she raised her hand to brush off some temporary blemish on her cheek, the catalyst of my floral associations became apparent in a stark reversal of image: the so-called "baby" orchid tied by a ribbon on her wrist, which I had purchased at some expense and which she now seemed to be pointing at me, I saw as the botanical impostor it was. It was more like one of those flesh-eating traps patiently waiting to ensnare. As I looked at it, its pollen-tipped tongue stuck out like a frog's, ready to suction bug, beast, or boy, it seemed silently to screech: *Nyahh! I'll get you before the night's over.*

The band took a break, and Charley, who ran the place, put a quarter in the juke box. I was right behind him and punched "Wish You Were Here," "Little Things Mean a Lot," "Love Is a Many-splendored Thing," and the latest one by The Hilltoppers. I left two for somebody else.

Ezra danced with Maureen, but they weren't what you might say getting the feel of things. Gracie and I polished off my selections in style, and I was tingling with my own charm. Then, when "Band of Gold" came on, I made a mental note about Ezra's ring as I dipped and glided about with moves that Long-Steppin' Sturgill might have envied. And after that one, as the Platters got into "Only You," I was commanding as a god. It wasn't just that I was swell; I was rhythmic and rhymed, a veritable ode in motion. On the merely sensual level, where all dull sublunaries dwelt, I was the white boy's answer to Mister Smooth—why, even to Cadillac Sam on a Saturday night. But on the lofty Plane of Art, where I longed to dwell, I wasn't just dipping with the best pair of legs the Kettle had ever seen. I was beyond Greek. I was Florentine. Immortal Dante. Why, I could have kept up with "Down Yonder" that night. I'd never die!

I returned Gracie, breathless (I assumed), to our booth; took up the shoe box with a clear indication that what was to follow was *men's* business; and with a wag of my head meant to convey, *Ah, Mister Tyler, shall we repair to the library for cigars and a snifter of brandy?*, I asked Ez if he'd like to join me in the men's room for a little pick-me-up.

We locked the door and took a pull on the Mason jar, and I saw his britches! Black cotton, knees like balloons, about three breaks at the shoe line. Dungarees, really, with cuffs! And his shoes? What he always wore: brown—or black?; heels worn even with the welt.

But he had a great grin on his face, and that I'd never seen.

After the second drink he told me he'd been in love with Maureen ever since second grade. "Man, she tears me up," he said, with a look of such sanguine mischief he seemed to be as proud of using a current expression—and that he *knew* it—as he was, finally, to have confessed to someone his long, abiding adoration. "Remember Waddle Goose?" He laughed.

"Sure do," I said, recalling the most egregious misnomer in the history of the county, with the possible exception of one of the Mullins boys, a 280-pound tackle with six broken legs to his credit. Snowflake's what they called him.

"When Maureen looked at him—." Ez didn't—or couldn't—finish it.

"When Maureen looked at him," I declaimed in my most solemnly romantic tone, "I heard her tresses stir upon my grave."

"Not bad," he said. "What's it from?"

"It's neo-me," I said.

"Sounds a lot like Poe," he said.

"Might just be," I said. "I'm getting where I can't always tell the difference."

Whereupon we discoursed, at short length, upon the lugubrious: ravens, premature burials, albatrosses, and Annabelle Lee.

"Wonder what ever happened to Bottle Juice?" He seemed determined to get back to what he had started all this talk with. "I mean, look at it like this: Uranus with his mother, for God's sake, begat Rhea. Rhea with her brother begat Zeus."

"Yeah," I said, and continued: "And old Zeus, with just about everybody else, *begat* just about everybody else, gods *and* mortals."

"Must have become pretty monotonous for him," Ez said.

"Why's that?" I said. "You can rest up in between."

"Well, he did sometimes change into animals," Ez said.

"I think that must have been for variety, or stealth," I said. "Why'd a woman ever think a swan or a bull might want to make out?"

"May just be he come to Colton six years ago in human form." He paused. "I mean, family name like *Zeus*? I been reading up on him some. He was sort of like a Olympian Zorro. Might strike anywheres, like the Big Z. Why, he had godkids with his mother, too. Sort of run in the family."

He seemed to be driving at something, so I let the pause ask what.

"No telling what he might've sired in these hills," he said.

"Ah, he's probably back in his courtyard," I said, lighting a cigarette and tired of the subject.

"Or a museum," he said. Then he smiled. "Good thing he didn't stay. Maybe even you'd have a hard time."

"What you mean by that there 'even'?" I said, switching to mountaineer.

"You're pretty low key tonight," he said.

"Funny, Ez."

"I mean, compared to usual," he said.

"I messed up with Rembrant," I said, but I didn't want to discuss it. "Hey, you got your ring?"

He tapped his chest. "Ri'cheer."

"Why don't you put it on?" I said.

He took off his clip-on bowtie, and I began to work on the collar stud, set with the others like rivets into a shirt that wasn't just starched—it was smelted. It could have repelled bullets.

When I finished, he reached up, rather casually and without a word, removed the cigarette from my lips, and...tossed it into the commode! As I stood there, wondering if he was going to say anything (he didn't), he found the chain around his neck and hoisted the ring. It was a beauty all right. Mine was a Cracker-Jack prize in comparison. As he put it on his finger, a little dirt under the nail, his face etched brightly with moonglow and moonshine and Maureen, I wondered if Gracie had neglected to wear Tommy Ray Sutliff's because of her low-cut dress or if, maybe, she was trying to tell me something.

"Flash it around, Ez," I said, buttoning him up. "And thump June Bug Hatcher on his fat head with it."

"Who gave the dough?" he said. "Come on."

"I'm sworn to secrecy, Ez. Really," I said, as my left hand reached into my pocket and gave him five of the six ones I had left, as if it—the hand—meant, on its own, to absolve me for what I'd "borrowed" from the ring funds and to clear itself of the rap it had taken for centuries for being sinister.

When it was accomplished, he said: "What's this for?"

"There was some left over," I said. "I got five, too, for when we go eat, after we...park." I whipped out the old Chapstick. I always carried it in my right front pocket (still do, but not for what I'm telling about here). I massaged, I lubricated—I meant to imbue those lips of mine so thoroughly with supple magic that, once touched by them, a novitiate would leap the nunnery's wall for more. I exaggerated it so that Ez would get the message about what was expected of him later: *to make out*. I blotted on a piece of toilet paper and asked him if my Chapstick was on straight.

He looked as if dementia had taken me.

"Just getting in kissing shape," I said, letting go of subtlety.

I think he blushed. But then he said, and it stunned me, "Right plain, ain't she?"

Plain? Beatrice awaited me in the next room. Plain!

A smile played slowly on his face. I'd been had. "Not bad, huh?" I said, taking a sip from the jar and passing it to him.

He shook his head and sort of whistled, raising the jar to his mouth. As the clear liquid touched his lips, he stopped and, just like that, dumped it into the commode! He flushed it, and in a voice unlike that of the Ezra Tyler I'd known, said, "We sure don't need any more of that, not with what we got."

I recalled what the cab driver had said, and I thought of Gracie's blinding beauty; that led me to Ezra's father on the corner, and the plunking of his banjo. "Sure...don't," I managed, watching about six hours in Gulf City's car wash swirl down the drain.

Then, as we crossed streams, he said, "Man, we sure are peers." And as we washed up and chewed sen-sen, I considered him, whom I had somewhat patronized. He had wit, humor, even irony—all the markings of a literary man. He lacked only hyperbole to join the pantheon of the Southern literati, but now that he had his girl that would follow nicely. And he knew his stuff. We were alike, in a lot of ways. He just lived a mile farther down the road.

"Okay, man," he said. "Gimme some skin!"

Like two cool hoods, we touched palms.

"Just ooooze it out, man," I said, and we laughed.

He pulled out the pocket Ingersoll and said, Britishly, "It's, ah, exactly nyun-thirty-two." Then he raised his leg and giving a mock kick at the door—and showing a red sock!—said: "Let's get back to the dames!"

He put his arm around my shoulder, and I did likewise.

"Thanks for everything," he said.

"Don't thank me, Ez. Pray for me."

He seemed to think it was a great joke.

As we pushed out the door, the band was playing "Tuxedo Junction," and I felt like the Student Prince, relieved for a time of his position and enjoying the revelry around him.

"*Then hey for boot and horse, lad / And round the world away....*"

It was difficult getting back to the booth. Everybody was crowded around, clapping and shouting. I turned with the empty shoe box under my arm, aping a fullback running backwards, while Ez pushed and followed. I felt the opening and saw the scowls on the faces of those we had jarred. And when I turned into the scene, the *cause célèbre*, there was Chief, dressed to the nines, doing the Varsity Drag with that month's eighth-grade English teacher. He was in rare form; his partner was his equal. I couldn't even clap time to the music with the others, I was so watchful.

When it ended, the syncopated clapping slid over into sustained applause. Those seemingly always mild-mannered women who came to the mountains to teach diagramming, parsing, and conjugation (of verbs) to hormonally delirious boys whose faces were pimpled like a crop of bean sprouts and whose major concern in class was a private game of pocket pool (and woe to any new woman, without Coach Carson's protection, who intruded before the *coup de grâce*)—such women were legion. This one was young and beautiful. I wondered if Chief had brought her to the dance or, since so many served as chaperones, had met her there.

He walked to the booth, where Ezra and I had gone, and introduced Miss Anderson. I was not going to be superficial and talk about his dancing (though I was still taken with the image of it). Besides, I was dizzy, in more ways than one. They were all chattering away, Gracie talking to "Marge," as Miss Anderson had told her to call her, Ezra and Maureen having made a breakthrough to casual speech, Chief talking to the lot of them as they turned remarks his way.

He was avoiding me, all right. Setting my mouth firmly and squinting my eyes, I looked at him as he lit a cigarette. In the flame, sweat shone from his brow and in the fine, black hairs of his temple.

"Monday, without fail," I heard.

I opened my eyes fully and blinked.

"Make an A and you get a C. Make a B, and it's a D. Anything else is an F." Then he added, with a slight turn of his head to let me know that while the breach had been serious, he knew I'd paid a price: "Fair enough, Tonio?"

My old spirit came twirling out of my body and shook hands with it. Then my mind returned, and all three were taking the hand of my master, who, with a bare nod to Ezra and Maureen, winked as if to say, *"Lord of yourself I crown and mitre you."*

❦ ❦ ❦

The music has ended; light precipitates The Last Groan. As the dancers retreat to the booths or stand there blinking as if such brightness does not belong in this world, Thurman Hatcher parades his unearned confidence for what will be the final time before his classmates in Colton. "May I have your attention, please?" he tries to command. The noise continues until somebody (probably J. Q. Risener, the only male old enough to portray the father convincingly in our senior play, *Cheaper by the Dozen*) whistles loud enough to call a horse from over a hill.

"Thank you," Thurman says to the anonymous whistler. "It is time to announce the King and Queen of the Prom. Fellow classmates, I give you Mister William Rembrant."

Applause. Somebody yells: "Way to go, June Bug. *Brilliant* innerduction!"

Then the Chief, impeccable in his dress and manner, is announcing members of the court: Sideliner girls, the token junior, relatively Mainstream escorts. A semi-circle forms around him before the dead fireplace, and I scour the remaining Sideliners for a king. It should be Peter the Mainstream Superlative, who has it all. As the queen should be Frances Freeman, or one of several other beauties with and without brains.

But since Chief has come to our town, and to our school, changes have been occurring. More and more the so-called fringe elements have been brought into the fold. In a reverse of tradition the Least Likely has become the Most. You could pick out the standard-bearers and discount them. At first, it seemed wrong-headed, but it has turned out to be, in many ways, the Perfect Solution. Rival girls have not had to vote for their worst enemy, then smile with Miss American hypocrisy during the crowning. It will be commoners all right.

"A king should be a man of quiet dignity," Chief begins.

I cannot of course be what he is saying, for I'm already an escort. Besides, I have other duties in the kingdom.

"This young man who has walked among you for twelve years has braved weather, of all kinds, to achieve perfect attendance the last two. Above all, he has a fine mind." Chief pauses, and with that smile of his that could light a boy's way for a long time, says—and I'm already looking at Ez—"Ladies and gentlemen, it is my pleasure to crown the King of the Prom, Ezra Tyler."

Now everyone seeks out old Ez, beet red as whenever anyone approaches him. But he rises to the applause and goes undaunted—in his white jacket and run-over shoes and long britches; there's no chance the socks will show—to beside Chief. As the crown is placed, he adjusts it with the hand that wears the ring, glinting like a maharajah's jewel.

And then Chief tells us what a queen should be, and that Maureen is one. I cannot see Ezra's face as she makes her way thickly, elegantly, to the waiting crown, which Chief gives to Ezra to place on her head.

More applause. Superlatives and Sideliners are conjoined. Chaperones smile. And the secret whistler gives the moment a series of staccato shrillings....

Cheers rocked the Copper Kettle that night, as Rembrant and Marge Anderson did some dancing that might still be talked about by those who were there. Maureen Mingus and Ezra Tyler could not be stopped. They even joined the rest of us in The Stroll. When "Good-night, Sweetheart" played and they could be seen in their crowns dancing close in a corner, in a sort of secular purging, and since some good had come of my sin, I forgave myself for covering up my error with the rings. But only a real shriving by Father Flowers, I knew, could fully assuage my guilt. In my behalf, I felt that I could tell him, in so many words, that a spring now flowed where a humbled prince had trod.

▸ ▸ ▸

As for me and Gracie?

Parked on the hill by the old water tower, the royal couple plighting their troth in the back seat, I played Paolo to Gracie's Francesca—but *after* the sinful pleasure, when they're in Hell paying for it—and I mean *played*: I had both roles.

You know already how tough she was. But she was in different settings then. Now, the dancing and noise and, essentially, the people were gone. She was talking about stuff that I could handle with one ear and a monosyllabic rejoinder every now and then, so, while WCVA played "Glow Worm" and "Side by Side" on the radio, I put the last of the poem together in my head: *"Young blood must have its course, lad, / And every dog his day."* And then: I began to conjure.

First, the lips. Mine, that is. (Hers would come in a bit, when I fixated on them.) They were worked as a farmer works good soil, and needed only love and care. I had them detach, in the way the old, old movie cartoons had, where they sang, then became the bouncing ball we'd followed; and I sent them out on recon.

But I called them back.

They hadn't had much practice lately, and I needed to hone them, to mold them into a relentless kissing machine; for I meant, in only minutes, to engage in labial combat on the magnitude of Lancaster rolling around with his company officer's wife on that foamy beach on Pearl, the coming war be damned. I began searching the radio for a change of mood and managed to dial through the static to *Randy's Record Shop* in Gallatin, Tennessee, and The Four Coins, assuring me in thrilling, though impotent, harmony that her kisses would take me where surreptitiously I had begun already to transport myself—to Shangri-La—by turning only my head 45 degrees to port and kissing the mouth I made with my fingers, left-hand version, while saying with my mind's-voice: *"Come on, and kiss me, Grace."*

She might have thought something was up, but I needn't have worried. I had telepathy in ENGAGE and all antennae extended: There was nothing there. She talked on about how she would likely follow her boyfriend (who had an athletic scholarship for mastering the newfangled one-handed jump shot) to "UK" (which is what she was already calling what I knew was the University of Kentucky but wanted in my cynical heart to misconstrue openly as the United Kingdom, but didn't)—all ploys, I assumed, to keep my sweaty hands off her. Randy's change of song made me feel like the *"one-eyed cat peekin' in a seafood sto'"* Big Joe Turner was singing about. Then when a Drifter started in about how he was going to get him *"some honey love"*— and *"in the middle of the night!"* (*Randy's* was true to its name)—Gracie shifted into high verbal gear and I was drooling into the now-parted digital mouth. *"I kiss the wall's hole,"* Thisbe's line read in my head, *"not your lips at all."* Ah, a pox on it! Would I become just one more breath mint to be teased, dissolved—nay, immolated—on the pink lingual altar within those devil lips of hers? (That Randy: I swear, "Kiss of Fire" came on right then.) The drool was approaching flood stage, but I figured if Bogart could make out, no sweat for any of us.

It was time.

Double the ides of May are come, Mauzy.

Si, streunse (jerk); *ma not-a gone.*

"Mmm-hmm," I said to something she said about Lexington, then stretch-yawned and put my right arm, crooked at the elbow, onto the backrest. I knew she knew what was coming; she just didn't know when. Good. I needed the element of surprise. I pulled my right hand back some, so it could slide across the top of the backrest, which is what it did, while my head turned for a quick finger-mouth peck. Seemed like my body parts (the unimportant ones) were acting on their own.

I could hear and feel her preparing for me. Her arms went up, as when a girl does one of those things with her hair meant to give a boy apoplexy, or when she…unhooks or…unbuttons something. My finger touched…neck, I supposed. But she kept talking. Good news in a sense; bad in another. I began sort of rubbing with my finger, so lightly I wondered if such delicacy could be perceived.

On the pretense of radio trouble, I leaned forward and, of course, glanced legward. There was such a sight being served up in the amber glow, I would have been content to dial through static forever to keep my gaze on the delicious curvature before me. But I was now craning, I knew, and so I turned back…into a flame! She released the trigger mechanism of what appeared to be a gold cigarette lighter and (odd, since she didn't smoke) drew once on a cigarette which she withdrew from her mouth and held before us like a miniature poker in line with my eyes. When I shifted my head, she followed with the red-hot coal. I felt like a cobra in thrall. She lifted her hand and drew on the cigarette again, and I saw on her wrist, eerily lighted by the glowing coal and coming slowly to focus through the shrouds of smoke, the killer orchid, patient and ugly as ever, and with a smile—it was more of a leer—on its…I can't say face…it was all mouth. About the only thing Greek left to me now was what the Cyclops must have thought at the moment of blinding.

But something about her had altered, I saw, as I pulled back and the smoke cleared. It seemed that her neck had been severed by a thick blade, her head hovering in place above the gash, and something shiny had come out of her throat just below—maybe it was—her Adam's apple.

When what had actually happened came clear, I realized what I was up against, and had been all night. For on a dark choker ribbon she had put her boyfriend's class ring around her neck and was now prepared, with the threat of instant blindness, to defend its symbolic fidelity.

Heavy necking sounded above the radio; Ez and Maureen had left off even coming up for air. I was paralyzed, not from fear, but because for the first time I not only did not know what to say or do; I didn't know what to think or dream up. And that's when I realized something else: that I often spoke, and thought, not for the meanings of words, but because they scanned. I was an anachronistic merchant of fluff.

I thought I heard: *leave me alone*. Maybe it was: *get out of town, you*.

"When do you leave?" she repeated. "I mean, for the university."

"Still have three months to go," I said. But that elicited no useful—rather, no—response.

"What you going to take up once you're there?" she said.

I coughed and whispered within a sigh, resignedly, "English."

Funny, now that I think about it, how much was at stake. Something momentous was being dealt with. Gracie Joyce Crowder and I, Antonio Lunkett Morelli, were sitting in the front seat of a 1947 Hudson, in the early-morning hours of May 31, 1956, near an old water tower in a small town in southwestern Virginia. I was much relieved that the news was out, since I had been feigning a passion for the sciences with her for some time.

And now she, whom I had held above all the stars in the Milky Way this night; she, who had been my muse of dance; whose loveliness and mere presence, I had thought all night, would keep even a middling poet inspired—she, Gracie Crowder, now chortled: "Guess I better watch my grammar."

She smiled then, rather inanely, and I saw back along the side of her teeth a dark spot that could have been anything: a filling, a shadow, a piece of grape skin, a peanut hull. I took it for rot.

She's-a no fer you.

It was Mauzy, getting the last word in, in my head.

And so in a moment, after all the manipulation, I was loosed from the human bondage I had been in the grips of all night. For now I knew that next to me sat, not Beatrice, over whom I had worked myself into something of a lather, flattering myself that I had been regaling the crowd with her for hours; nor even her earthly form in the guise of a Harlan cheerleader. I was up against *la belle dame sans merci* herself! I didn't know now whether to try to nuzzle that still gorgeous neck, or throttle it. But of course I did neither. She knew she was safe, and had been all along.

Ah, she was a year older than me anyway. Which of course brought to mind the only half-a-poem I had in my head. To have recited *something splendid*—the young half—would have been like speaking out at her wedding when the Baptist preacher called for objections. But I wish now that I had memorized the second stanza, in elegiac cadences. I just might have risked that one.

But Chief had always said to treat the girls like ladies and the boys like gentlemen, unless they proved otherwise. While Gracie had lighted a cigarette, she didn't exactly smoke; she had bad teeth, maybe, but even a lady could have missed a dental appointment. Anyway, now that I was back in Chief's good graces, I could afford to be magnanimous. But I had only a buck to my name, and that time had approached when a hot dog and a bowl of mushroom soup and a Pepsi were the world's great reality before dawn. If Lady Grace possessed a more refined palate, I'd have to borrow a little from Ez. New Ez. I could just hear him: *Here, you mooch.*

And so, with such mundane thoughts the night was coming to a close. Mauzy's prophecy notwithstanding, I had not exactly received more than I had wanted. But I had had a "plendy good time," on the dance floor and in my head. And I sure had watched out all right. When it had counted, I literally had not touched the girl, only the ribbon.

But what did I know? I was seventeen, with no idea that the man I might someday want to be was somehow related to William Rembrant. I would never have thought that in two-and-a-half years from that night, an otherwise buoyant Saturday morning at the university—a beautiful, crisp fall day, the stuff of which football is made—would be turned into the bluest Sunday with the news of Chief's death.

Of course I would not have. I had started up the Hudson and was turning down the hill on my way to the Colton Cafe, lost again in poesy, adrift in the empyrean, dreaming already of the pretty yellow-haired girl with blue eyes, the one my grandmother, who had never failed me yet, said some day I'd marry.

Man of Letters

Man of Letters

I suppose that, in a way, I attempted to arrange a meeting with Andrew because I needed to impress you. If you remember, it had been quite some time since I had been in your good graces, so to speak, and I thought that seeing him again with you and the children there would be just what I—just what we—needed. I had no idea that it was going to turn out the way it did, though I was fairly certain that you would see him in the light I always wanted you to. Little did I know at the time that your point of view would simply be reinforced, that what I began as a kind of reconciliation would turn out to be my undoing.

The last time we saw him together he stayed at the house with us. It was before Andy was born, so it had been six or seven years. I myself had managed in the interval only one meeting with him: when he was in Washington for the Library of Congress Writers' Conference. I can recall that meeting as plainly as the day Andy was born. There he was—Andrew Porter—just the right age for his reputation which, with his *Selected Stories*, exceeded by far any exalted notion even I might ever have had. Everybody at the conference seemed to defer to him; his name was mentioned I don't know how many times, nor by how many critics and other writers, as the best writer—or one of the best—in the country. And throughout it all I was keeping steady company with him.

I had arrived early and had found him in the coffee shop of his hotel. (He'd written me where he'd be staying.) After breakfast—his; I'd already had mine—he said, "Let's go shopping." As we walked around, I hoped that we might be able at last to play a game of rotation pool. It had been a little thing between us, ever since my days in Arundeltown. But we passed no pool rooms, and I took no occasion to suggest that we might seek one out, frankly because it came to me that I could not recall with any certainty if he had intended back when I was a student that we should play billiards, or common pool—the kind they play where I come from.

Then we came to the clothing store, and I busied myself while he selected a jacket. He had on a perfectly good seersucker, but he told me that he had come to Washington between trips and had been unable to pack fresh clothing or to have a few things pressed. (It's very odd, now that I think of it, to imagine that Andrew Porter quite possibly walked the streets that day with a soiled collar.) When he began to write out a check, the clerk told him that out-of-town checks were not accepted, and so I volunteered to put the jacket on our charge card and let Andrew write the check to me. He hadn't, for some reason, a credit card of his own. He was pleased, it seemed, that I made the matter simpler than it might otherwise have been, though, secretly, I thought that he was a bit embarrassed by it all. I wanted to tell the clerk who he was, but I checked (ha-ha) the impulse. Had you and I been better off financially in those days, I would have kept the check as a memento, but of course I finally did deposit it in our account, after I photocopied it.

That evening, several of us piled into our car, for I was the only one living near enough, then, to have brought one. I drove them—John Jordette, Rocko Janise, Andrew, and a scholar from Kentucky named Mandrake—to a restaurant for dinner. Somewhere along the way I stopped for gas, and we all got out of the car while a black boy (a real *boy*, in age) filled up the car. Then when I was paying him, he looked over at Andrew and said, "Man, you sure got the boss coat in *that* car."

The jacket *was* quite elegant, in a simple way, in the best way, that is. We all broke up laughing, as we drove on, and the heavily Southern group of them began to talk in their thick accents (mine, as you know, is mountain) about that "boss coat." I recall that Mandrake, trying, it seemed, to be more of the group than he was, said: "Just think: Now they'll send that boy to Harvard some day and we'll never hear such a marv'lous phrase from him again. 'Boss coat!' Cain't ever beat *that!*"

Later, over drinks and cigarettes at the restaurant, when the talk was flowing and who knew but that little legends were being laid, I said during a lull that the waitress sashayed prettily.

"Gabe, you're common," Andrew said with a smile, and we all laughed.

So I suppose that on that day that you and the children and I went to Arno, I was full to bursting with my memories of him. You remember how it was back in my hometown, visiting my relatives after a trip half way across the country. I was beside myself with boredom, what with renewing old acquaintances and seeing all of my aging aunts and uncles and trying to distinguish younger cousins from one another—and I wanted us to visit Andrew and Helen in their eighteenth-century house. He had written about it in one of his letters a good time before. I wanted the children, especially Andy, to see my old college town and meet my renowned teacher and perhaps be held by him on his lap. Who knew how long he might live? He had been ill, I had learned, and he was getting on in years. I wanted Andy and little Marie to know somebody I had been close to as a student and then, later, as a friend. (I thought of him, in the old sense, as my master.) I suppose that I wanted them, and you, to be near him because I felt so near to him. I imagine that you must see it as a failing in me, but I have always been taken by such men as Andrew. I admit as much. They seem so self-possessed and know so well what they are about.

In any event, I had pretty much had my fill of reminiscing in Arno. Do you remember asking me where I had been on the morning, very early, that we left? It was when I returned and woke you for our return trip back home, and you were surprised that I was dressed and seemed to have come from out-of-doors. Well, I *had* been outside already, though I avoided talking about it at the time, then avoided it altogether thereafter. I didn't want you to think that I was still sentimental about the place. But I had re-traced that morning a walk I had taken a long time ago, on another early-morning odyssey about my town. It had been some seventeen years before, on the morning that I had left home for college, thinking then that I had to go on and become an engineer.

In my re-tracing, I tried again to see everything I had seen on that other morning. I even wandered into one of my old school buildings, by a back door this time...only it was no longer a school but some sort of federal building, social security or somesuch, badly neglected and with the upper floor of what was once the elementary school's auditorium closed off. I exchanged a few words with the custodian, a young man with a bandit's mustache like so many of them wear today, and almost made the mistake of asking him if he were the "janitor."

The old sixth-and-seventh-grade building (we had called it, fondly, The Barn) was not there at all, except in my head. There was only gravel on the spot where as a boy I had played out my adolescent dramas. And the high school—one could, back then in Arno, go from kindergarten through high school on a single block—the high-school building was shut up altogether, the windows boarded over.

I left that scene and went to the swimming pool, but when I remembered what was there—or what was not there—I paused only long enough to see the caved-in stones, still, though faintly, aqua-colored, like idle boulders for a road gang's work. The bathhouse was toppled, and one of the two old giant spigots once used to fill up the pool was stuck atop a pile of debris like a ninety-degree chimney. The whole thing was like a graveyard of forgotten youth, and I turned away from there.

I looked for old landmarks, aging bums, sidewalks cracks, anything I might once have thought essential to hold in my head forever. I even returned to the real graveyard on Laurel Hill, to try to find the resting places of my kinsmen. But even the oak tree on the hill behind the old house was nothing more than a decaying stump. Everything had shrunken…but anyway, I wanted after I woke you to get on with a different sort of visit.

You had said, as if you really didn't know I had been out already, "Are we in a hurry?" I suspect you were referring, good-humoredly, to my travel habits back then, when I might delay us till noon. Well, I wanted to put the right flavor of topping on our return, to stop and chat and have, perhaps, a glass of sherry and to sit in Andrew's light while you and Helen and the children either joined us or else walked in the garden or prepared a meal. I did think, before I learned of their move, that we would be invited to take lunch with them. I wanted to ask him all sorts of questions about his stories, questions that for some reason or other I had failed to ask when I was his student and had so many opportunities to do so. But I suppose it is natural that, back then, I was more concerned with my own stories than with his. I wanted him to sign his marvelous *Selected Stories* while the two of us sat in his study. And as you know, for I told you, I wanted to apologize, if that is the word for wanting to set right a mild statement of criticism—I wanted to make amends for that unfortunate sentence I wrote when I reviewed his novella, *Remembered Kin*, where I said, and I quote: "If this novella does not get the reception it deserves, it might be because a large reading public will not feel completely at home in Andrew Porter's characters' homes." Well, *you* know what I meant by that. It was not written to cast aspersions on Andrew, nor on Helen. I merely meant to suggest that even full-scale novels that sell well today cannot have opulent trappings, not important novels, that the serious reading public is out of sorts with that kind of setting in our day and age, and that—and here was my true meaning—and that Andrew Porter *deserves* more attention from a larger public. A hopeless situation, I now see, because there is no large serious reading public. It is not enough that a man who writes such brilliant stories be admired merely by other writers and critics. Who, after all, would want to be known as a so-called writer's writer? If the people would read him, I felt, even though they might not connect with his settings they might be better off for having lived vicariously the lives of his characters.

But you know all of that. I have told it to you so many times. You know how I feel—truly feel—about his work, and I think that you must share my feelings. I remember that you said on more than one occasion that Andrew writes very delicately and perceptively from the woman's point of view. I guess that I am trying, in a way, to explain to you, and to myself, just how and why I became so influenced by Andrew and why, that hot and muggy day, I had such a need to impress you and to sit in his shadow once again. (I see that his "light," above, has changed to "shadow" now. I suppose that this could be some sort of pathetic fallacy in me.) I do not expect that you will fully understand—nor that you will agree—but that is my urge: to set the record straight on this matter once and for all.

Now I know that you have a different opinion, that in your eyes it was not the review itself that might have turned him against me, but that he and I were—and always will remain—from worlds-apart cultural backgrounds, that our friendship was transient by its nature, and that perhaps he simply did not care as much as I. But I was, and still am, in a way, rather proud of that review. In it, I praised him for all of his past work, I looked forward to his future work "with great promise," and finally I gave the book a highly favorable review. Still, I had to say something objective, something other than approving. Everyone would surely know that I had been his student, was now his friend. What else could I do? And to tell the truth, I suppose that I meant the statement literally as well as in the other ways I mentioned earlier. Certainly I mean it now, or will by the time I finish this, though so much has changed since I wrote it and came to regret it.

Or it could have been the anthology I put together. I had selected one of his stories for it, of course. What story collection could be said to be complete without one by Andrew Porter? But then my editor thought it much too long and not quite right for the type of student coming along. You must remember how that "era" was. I could have insisted on it, I suppose, but in the end, of course, I deferred to the editor. After all, it was my first (and, still, only) book; I didn't want to jeopardize its potential by having my editor down on it from the onset. For the same reason, I didn't even try to include one of my own stories.

Andrew Porter's story may not have been right for the times. (Perhaps there was perception of truth in my critical statement about his "characters' homes" after all.) But, if so, it was merely because it was too *good* a story. In the end, though, I had to leave it out. But that could not have been the reason for his disaffection. He isn't small about such things, surely. No, that could not have been it.

You were not, of course, with me when I met with him as a student keeping an appointment with his writer-professor. I used to look forward all week to those meetings. We met on Thursdays, I recall, just before you came home from work, and every appointed day I would buy two small bottles of Coca-Cola, the old size that used to be fifteen cents, ice-cold from that little store on Grace Street, where we shopped for holiday meat. I am sure you must remember it. I would take the soft drinks, along with a copy of my manuscript, to that old Victorian house across from the university where Andrew had likely written several of his stories and which served as his office. I did not then, of course, call him Andrew; it was not until just before graduation that he told to call him by his first name, but even now I don't feel at ease doing so. I remember that I said, jokingly, of course: "That's only as it should be. After all, I now have a master's degree; you have only a bachelor's." We laughed together. It was at our writing seminar's final dinner party at the big house they had then, where you first met Helen. (And then there was the party we had at our house. I invited Andrew, though you didn't think he'd come, but he showed up and you did the Charleston with him.)

It was strange to be walking "roads" and "ways" with names like Gloucester and Stranum. I half-expected at any turn to find myself on the Appian Way or Banks-of-Thames Lane, as if Arundeltown were some lesser London, or Rome. For I had been accustomed, in Arno, to Oak and Pine, to Fourth and the likes of Mullins—and always with a simple "Street" tag, except for our main, called of all things Madison Avenue. I puzzled over what I was doing in such a setting; it seemed so…historical. But then inadequacy seemed always to pass so that, by the time I turned onto Dunedin Road, with its dogwood and rhododendron, I felt as if I carried the very cup of trembling on my ascent of Parnassus.

Within his office of that old house we would sit for what seemed like hours, beginning at first a detailed discussion of my story. But then, inevitably, something—a character, a scene—would appeal (I flatter myself, I know, to suppose this the word)—would touch something in him and we would forget the manuscript before us and simply talk: about my crude beginnings in Arno or perhaps some renowned friend of his whose very name (he did not usually give it; I had to ask) made the hairs on my arms stand to attention. I would look at the photographs on the wall above his desk—Henry James, Chekhov, only a few others—and feel something pass from them, through him, to me. Later, much later, I sent him, on a lark one day, a picture of myself when I was a boy and had imitated Al Jolson (you know the one) on the stage of the Koltown Theater in Arno. I learned that he added my picture to that august gallery above his desk, the only student picture he ever displayed. Then when the discussion was over, he would cap his fountain pen (while I wished I had never given up my own), and sometimes he would give me a ride home on his way to his own house on Worcester Drive. (You even said, after several of these rides, "He likes you.")

He said on one of those occasions in his office, and I can see now the slight twist of his mouth as he said it, in that way he has of animating his spoken words with his lip movements: "Gabe, you have a raw material in you like a mother lode. Not any of the better writers in class—those better right now, that is—will last because they will write themselves out. You will have to work harder at the writing, to develop your own style, but when you do—and you will—you will be head and shoulders above them all." He said this to me as we sat there near the end of it all, poring over my story, that long one called "Before We're Old"—remember? He was in his shirtsleeves in an intoxicating suspension of propriety, and I felt unstoppable, chosen. I was going to eclipse them all. All I had to do was develop my style, then select at will from my inexhaustible store of recallable material. Oh, yes, and he said on another occasion, I remember: "I envy you your background. It is one thing to be white, Anglo-Saxon, and Protestant in the South and to be a writer; but to be Italian-American, Roman Catholic, and a Southern writer—ah, that's the best of all worlds." He said this after several cocktails at a party. Then he added, laughing, "Of course, it wouldn't hurt to have an idiot in the attic, either."

It happened that he said that—about my "raw material"—at about the time that William Pruett—a close friend of Andrew's from as far back as their college days, whose picture hung between Katherine Anne Porter's and Chekhov's—came to the university to read and to visit our class. That made the comment especially sweet because I walked along with Messieurs Pruett and Porter through the hallways that day and ended up in the elevator between them. They were both surprisingly large, even athletic-looking men, and I felt their polish on both my sides. Something about each man was unusual: shoes, shirt, jacket. Pruett wore an ascot, though it was rumpled rather badly. But it was more than mere clothing. Pruett's New-England eloquence; Porter's soft, Southern cadences—as they chatted amiably, I watched the door like an elevator operator of old, my ears feeding on the music those men made.

Then suddenly Andrew said, "Mister Giacone here is one of our more promising fiction writers, Cab," and I stole a direct look up into the bulging eyes beneath William Pruett's spectacles. His brooding intelligence was formidable; his hair seemed itself to be brains. I could almost hear the anapests of his legendary poem about the whales, and I am certain that my face flushed as I thought about my own secret raw material, then tried to comport myself with an extra measure of dignity out the elevator door, after my elders, my betters.

I do not tell you these things because I think that I have actually fulfilled all, or even any, of my so-called promise, as a writer or as a husband or father. I suppose that these things are all too mixed up in me for me to be able even to approach a realization of them all. But what I wanted to tell you about was that day that I insisted—I admit that I did insist, in my own way—that we stop by to see the Porters.

❦ ❦ ❦

Do you remember the conversation as we were winding down our visit in Arno, the talk turning as it always does when one returns to his hometown—that talk by the older relatives about how I was when I was a boy—as if I existed in their minds as only a boy? There was nothing at all about what I had done since I had left, nothing whatsoever of my having earned two degrees or that I had written anything. And they—all of them—knew that I had just published a story. After all, I had gone to the trouble of sending each of them a copy.

I realize that some of this might sound small of me, but I had a vision of much of my work's being set in and around Arno. I wanted it to be my exclusive fictional domain, so to speak. I wanted to bring to that region a measure of some attention, perhaps even make known some of the poor conditions in those ever-darkening Cumberland Mountains. And then to find out that no one seemed even to have read my first story was, frankly, a blow. Perhaps I do expect too much from people, as you have told me so often. I guess that, yes, in a way, I wanted a lot from them. But I was also willing to give as much, or more. I was willing and, I think, able to deal with Arno and that part of Appalachia as a regional writer would, though with more to offer, so that "mere regionalism" would not be invoked in possible reviews I might myself get. I expected, in short, what I was perfectly willing to return: attention, concern, knowledge, even respect. But then, you have now told me that my attention to that area is self-motivated, that I live in the past, that my concern is really anger, though my knowledge is true. It seems to me, then, that you are saying that I am a knowledgeable, though angry, egotist.

Be that as it may. I called Andrew to let him know that we would be driving through Arundeltown the next day. I recall his saying, "Tomorrow, we depart for something more manageable in our encroaching dotage," meaning the smaller house, of course. Then he added, giving me the new address, "By all means, do stop by."

Surely, you must have known that I had your interests in mind as well as my own, for you would have been able to see some of Helen's latest paintings. I had envisioned her taking you to her studio, perhaps encouraging you to return to your own brushes. I had it in mind, too, that I could perhaps help them move, or arrange their furniture, that then we could have ordered something from a carry-out restaurant and had just a casual lunch in their back yard. Certainly when I found out about the move I did not expect Helen to prepare anything for us. I wanted them to understand that what was important was our seeing one another and that the condition of their house was not something that we would likely be uneasy about.

Now, of course, I did not actually say any of this. In the back of my mind was the apprehension that our being half a continent away would end everything with them if the four of us did not make a special effort to visit when we were near enough to do so—as we were. "By all means, do stop by": It was a perfectly clear invitation.

And so we did.

▸ ▸ ▸

But let me digress a moment before I get to that part of the story. I want to say just a few things about the letters I received from Andrew.

At first, they were longish, personal letters equal, almost, in number and even length to those I wrote to him in that first year after I left the university. Of course, at first I had to write him for various letters of recommendation. I was, at that time, always applying for teaching jobs, as you know too well, trying to improve our situation so that I could write more and we could live more comfortably. And I know that he sent letters in my behalf to the places I asked him to. Of course, I did not want to intrude on his time, for I know how it is when you are trying to write and teach and you have students making constant demands on you. Anyway, he did those things for me. He wrote the letters.

And he wrote to me about his own work, about Helen's paintings and occasional one-woman shows, about how the students had changed since I had left the university, and generally about things that friends say to each other in such letters. Invariably, he would say something about dropping by to see him when we were in the area again; and, while they may not have been in-depth letters with formal invitations to do so, still he said those things. And I took him at his word, as a gentleman. It was a back-and-forth, you-now-owe-me-one sort of correspondence, as it should have been. He even wrote to me when his father died and he had to cancel the reading I had set up for him at my college, and it was a letter I will always keep and remember. For it was quite a blow to him. I never bothered to write to him when my father died, not because I did not want to, but because, as you know, my father was nothing like a Porter and died under circumstances altogether different, even bizarre. Frankly, I was embarrassed about the entire ordeal, from the notification of death to the strange, closed-casket funeral. Besides, my father and I had been estranged for years. But then all of that is another story, which you know already. Suffice it to say that I felt uneasily privileged when Andrew confided in me about how much his father had meant to him. I was in my early thirties, feeling sympathy for a man in his fifties, a man old enough to be my father, who had lost his father, who, in turn, must have been eighty. But then, I certainly think that such sympathy is as it should be between friends.

Then he was kind enough to read and respond to the manuscripts I sent him. You probably think I was forcing myself on him, but you perhaps do not understand that this sort of thing is done among writers. The student-teacher relation ends, but then a writer-to-writer friendship gets established, and so formal instruction is replaced by support. Surely Andrew had his own literary fathers when he was a young man. I imagine that those famous friends of his—and they were quite a collection of luminaries—must have been gratified to have discovered and helped his talent along. If I am ever in the position to do so, I too will feel obliged—no, honored!—to help my own former students get established.

I maintain, however, that the letters stopped after he must have read the review. There was no other reason for it to have happened; and, believe me, I have considered it from all angles. Things changed with that review; I am now certain of it. With one sentence an entire friendship was essentially terminated. I would guess that your position is that if a friendship goes sour because of such a "petty" detail, then it was not true in the first place. And this is where we differ, for it—the friendship—was true all right. It must just have been that I wrote it at a bad time in his life. Or perhaps his own two sons were growing into an age where he could talk to them as he had once talked to me and that he no longer needed a surrogate son, if that is what I was to him for a short time. He was married late in life, you know. Moreover, there was still the fact that while other writers and the best critics praised his work, he did not receive, as I wrote, "the popularity he deserves."

Whatever the case, by the time we drove up to the smaller, circa 1920s, house they had moved to that morning, the letters had ceased altogether.

❦ ❦ ❦

Let me now try to take you back so that I may give my version of the events of that day.

It was, while excessively hot, the most sublime of afternoons, and as we passed the university on our way through town I had the pain of recollection which I will never forget. My sessions with Andrew were, as I have described them, enjoyable and inspiring. But the remembering that day—the moment when I gazed at the campus and saw a younger version of myself, strolling along with one of the best writers in the country—the recollection was even more sublime than any actual weather. Recall that it was not yet officially summer. Already, though, that landscape was ablaze with color, intoxicating with scent. In that moment, with the remembrance, I had another realization: I wanted desperately to become established enough so that I might one day teach on that campus with Andrew Porter. I realized, further, that no place could compare to the beauty and serenity we were passing at that very moment.

So as we drove on, I remember my spirit's being especially buoyed by the vision and then alternately let down because of its being only a vision, a hope. I know that this is not making perfect sense to you. I am trying to go beyond the mere externals and get to the substance of my mind during that day's events. My own theory about writing, such as it is, is that one must be true to one's own self before it can ever follow that a reader will connect with it. There must be, above all else, sincerity in the writing, and the only way to be sincere, in my scheme of things, is to show the conditions under which a scene takes place. For me, it is not enough merely to present the scene, though it seems more and more to be the modern way.

But before you say it, let me: What about your own frame of mind that day? How about the conditions under which you experienced those events? Well, again: That is the writer's job, to transfer himself imaginatively into other people's bodies and minds. Was I, then, in yours that day? And the honest truth is that, no, I was not—not then. But I am now, as I look back, and I am going to try to describe the scene partially from your own angle of vision.

I have come to know that much of what we experienced together while I was at the university was more one-sided than I would ever have admitted, that you were not all that taken by Yorkshire County, Virginia, nor the people within it. Now, of course, we do know that that was the case; back then, I would not have guessed it. So be it. But that was the frame of your mind, as I now perceive it, as we drove through that part of the country that was, finally by then, foreign to your sensibility. I have often wondered what must have gone through your mind on all the other occasions when you were face-to-face with mountaineers and coal miners and even reprobates and drunks in Arno. Surely, you had "escaped" that side of life where you were raised, at least from what I have seen of it. But then, I have to wonder even more about your feelings concerning the so-called gentry of Yorkshire County. And that is where I am, frankly, at a loss.

I know that you have thought that my dreams of success and my yearning for acceptance by people like Andrew and Helen Porter have been idle dreams, delusions of grandeur. I deny that. They are not by any means idle, nor even unrealistic. Didn't Helen herself suggest that we—the four of us—all go to Europe together someday, or perhaps meet there? Now you may have taken her suggestion as a piece of idleness on *her* part. I did not. She surely is not one to say something like that and not mean it. You may be thinking that she said it only to be kind, to be making conversation, because we were at her house and I was Andrew's student. Just because I am not of these people does not mean that I cannot become their friends. Artists, after all, are blind to class—at least the true ones are, and there are no other kinds. I think that you will have to agree with me on this point even if you disagree on all others: The Porters *are* consummate artists. Aristocrats or not—I meant to be counted among their friends.

It was simply a shame that it had to turn out the way it did, but I still believe that it was a professional—a literary—misunderstanding rather than one of class.

▸ ▸ ▸

But back to that day.

Andy was awake. You and Marie in your arms were lightly asleep. (I remember it as an almost madonna-and-child scene.) I will never forget what I said to Andy as I looked at him in the rear-view mirror. We were nearing Arundeltown, cruising down the highway after the breathtaking curviness and beauty of the mountain, and I said: "Slick your hair down, Son. You're going to meet a good friend of mine. He used to be my teacher, and he's one of the best writers in the whole world."

"What for?" Andy said. You know how he is. His precocity would not allow him simply to acquiesce. In that respect, I was a bit proud of his independence in asking the question. How is he?

"You'll see. You'll see," I said. "You're going to meet the man you were named for."

It must have passed over his head. Probably, he was off in the clouds. Namesake to Andrew Porter, he was as innocent about it as if he had been named after one of my uncles.

Then I began to wonder about his rejoinder—"What for?"—and it occurred to me that he might have been asking why he should slick down his hair rather than why he was going to meet Andrew. And then it came to me that he was questioning the essence of the imperative itself. I had not used—had not even heard—that expression in years. (And I had never used "Son" to address him, as I would never expect him at some point to come to address me as "Father," both terms used often in Andrew's stories.) It was just something that came out of me, from out of my own past, and I rather liked having dredged up that little piece of memory. I fancy that little Andy Porter's father might very well have said something like that to him on a similar occasion back in his past.

It might even have been something that I had subconsciously tucked away for just that moment.

In any event, it sounded just right and I followed through with the gesture. I licked my fingers, reached back across the seat, and slicked down Andy's cowlick. He cowered at my touch, though, showing his disgust at having spit put on his hair. And then I remembered that I, too, had cringed at such abominations when I was a boy. And that is when you awoke with a start, asking straight off, "What's the matter? What's *wrong?*" You must have thought we were going to crash in that brief moment that I reached back and the car swerved ever so slightly.

"Nothing's wrong," I said. "But we're getting near. Better get ready."

You have always appreciated, or so I have thought, my waking you as we approach various towns, preparing for a stop or a visit with some relative or acquaintance. I recall your anxiety, your anticipation, on most of those approaches, and they all merge into one scene: Coming out of sleep, you bat your eyes awake, sit up, direct the children, put down the sun visor on your side to see yourself in the little mirror I clipped on the back for you, and make yourself up. You brush or comb your hair and put on lipstick and move about with some regard for whatever diner or rest stop or house we might be on the verge of entering. But not that day. That day, of all days, you sat looking at the dashboard, or just above it. You turned your head to look out the side window, and I tried to catch the reflection of your face in the glass because I had the odd notion that you might be crying, that your face might by then have been showing anger or scorn for what we were about to do.

At any rate, you did not begin to freshen up until I turned the car off the highway and began to drive through the streets of Arundeltown. And I remember then that you turned from the window with something like resignation showing on your face. By then Marie was awake and you managed to get her to go into the back with Andy, where they began immediately to scuffle and play. That seemed to leave us alone with ourselves, not just in the front seat, but in the very car. Something was passing between us, and I could not for the life of me understand why it had to be that way on what could have been a wonderful return to my college town.

Then, you will recall that I drove, not directly to the Porters', but to our very first house, on Sycamore Street. It was a more-or-less automatic reaction, I suppose, not one calculated to do whatever it is you may think I devised for effect. I simply drove to the house where we had lived for two years while I was at the university. And again, I remember the look on your face, though in this case your implacability did not reveal itself as anger or remorse or resentment at something in our past together. I suppose, on reflection, that as I parked there in the cul-de-sac, looking on at the little rambler with that sapling I planted, now high as the roof, you must have recalled either a wistfulness for the house and our life in it, or else a feeling that you had given up something when we left it for my first teaching job. I would like to think that it was the former, that even though we had lived in a blue-collar (though largely racist) neighborhood, the house was a symbol of our good, and younger, times and that the entire time back then was to you a memory of my own personal and professional growth. Whatever the case, you seemed none too happy to be parked there looking on at the house; and, if you remember, you let me know by saying, far too abruptly, "Let's go."

I thought that inconsiderate of you, especially concerning the children, and I said, "That's where Mommy and I lived when I was at the university, kids."

But they did not hear, or if they did they were too busy to respond.

The questions is: Why were you put off? If I had done something that I should not have done, why didn't you simply tell me? And if you were angry about something, why were you? What was it? People visit old places all the time.

But of course we drove on, and by then I, too, became moody and none too excited at our imminent visit with the Porters. You might say that by looking on at our own former little house and your reaction to it I became, like you, depressed. So by the time we arrived at the Porters' new address, I was almost hoping that they would not be there.

And at first I thought that I might have got my wish. You sat in the car while I let the children out in the yard to play. I had parked near the entrance of the driveway, and I can still hear the crunch of gravel as I began to walk to the house. It's strange how such sounds stay with me. While I should have felt—while I wanted to feel—like the prodigal returned to receive his patrimony, or some small gift, at least, I had no such feeling.

I say "I should have felt," because of what Andrew had said to me about my potential and because of something that happened at that Washington Conference. There were several of us there from my old writing seminar. A few of them, by the way, had already published a novel or a collection of stories or a book on some occasional topic; several had published stories in magazines. One was even an editor of a prominent journal. When one of my former classmates—the only one who had had no success so far, besides me—introduced me to Evan Godsey, she said that Godsey had been in and out of our seminar during our time there. He looked familiar, but I could not recall his presence in that class, and I told her—and him—so. Then Godsey, a strikingly handsome young man, blond and muscular, moved out of range in his tailored jacket and slacks, and Shirley Hanson said, "Oh, my, yes. He was Andrew's golden boy."

"Well, he could not have been there with us then," I said.

"Why not?" She had a wry smile on her face.

"Because I was."

No, that is not right. I did not say it in that way. I had had a drink or two or I would not have said what I actually said, not in the common expression I used.

"No way." That is what I really said. And I was mortified as soon as the words were out of my mouth, for they seemed clearly to contradict the very point I was trying to make with her.

I tried to recover. "He might have been the golden boy in looks," I said with a grin of my own, "but I was in the way that counted."

She didn't seem to understand.

"Mister Porter told me so," I added.

Why, Evan Godsey was not there during my time. Shirley Hanson must have had a thing for him.

In any event, I recall trying for some odd reason to cushion my steps in the Porters' gravel. Then I walked the stone path to the front door. What you do not know is that I looked back at you just before I lifted the brass knocker—much too large for that door, though of course their present house was hardly a cottage—that before I so much as touched that shiny knocker, I had a fleeting urge, even then, and then again with it poised and ready for striking, to gather up the children and drive with them and you away from there forever. I tell you this now not because I wish to transfer to you and your mood of that day some sense of guilt or responsibility for what happened—or, more accurately, for what did not happen—but because I want you to know that I am, that I was even at that late moment, capable of turning heel at the very door of the likes of the Andrew Porters when it comes to our own welfare.

Nonetheless, I rapped the oversized knocker, twice. I was still reeling from the image of your face as I turned back to the door, and yet I tried to reassure myself that we should be there and that in only minutes you, too, would feel as I did. I had been at that door—or, rather, at their other doors—several times before, of course; and always on those other occasions I had had the sense of being welcome, except when I was traveling through alone that time, even before the review, and I was told that Andrew was occupied with a guest. That time, Helen remembered me and was apologetic, though she seemed ill-at-ease with having to explain something so unnecessary. (That is what I understand least about people like the Porters. In their world, one has to call ahead. And so, this time, I had.)

The door opened a bare crack, the eyes of Helen Porter looked out at me, and the voice below them said: "Yes?"

Only that: "Yes?"

I remember distinctly that upon hearing the word I knew that I had made a mistake in coming, and, for whatever reason, two thoughts came simultaneously, or as nearly so as is possible to my mind. The first was that, as the door opened a bit farther, I was struck by the relatively youthful comeliness of a woman some twenty years your elder. At the same time that her face revealed itself to me by degrees, there being a fierce play of shadow in the dappled light, I looked down at the door's brass threshold. I did not remember her very well, I then realized, but moreso was I shaken by the apparent fact that she seemed not to recognize me. I suppose that, to be truthful, I expected the door to swing wide—yes, I had anticipated being let in with at least some fanfare, with Andrew somewhere behind her, calling, *Why, Gabe, come in*, and Helen going out to greet you and the children and bid you all come in.

Of course, no such thing happened. I had come to the very gate, only to go unheeded.

But then, oddly, the other thought that came to me was the picture of little Falstaff back in the kennel where we had left him for the week. I think that I must have heard his whine in that moment. I must have realized that I had left a creature I loved penned up while I was standing on the Porter doormat being spoken to as if I were a solicitor.

I tried to sound casual. "Hi, Helen," I said, smiling much too broadly, I am sure, for the occasion.

Still, she did not call me by name, saying only, "Oh, hello." Then she added, and I thought that it sounded abrupt, "Andrew is upstairs, lying down. He is not feeling well. I am doubtful that he is up to receiving anyone today."

I was faintly aware of the sounds the children were making. It occurred to me that I had taken the liberty of letting them intrude into the Porter yard, that they might at that very moment have been desecrating a rosebush or trampling newly sown seeds. And I was paralyzed with the prospect of having to turn from that door without as much as another word, without having been let in, with having to walk back to the car and your look and the two-days-long silent drive back home.

Mercifully, she added, "Step in, won't you? I will go up and see."

I entered what I called in my mind the vestibule. When she shut the door, I hoped that you would more or less assume responsibility for the children because I did not dare take the liberty of having them enter with me. I thought of all of this, and of some of the trappings of the Porter stories. Words like portico and balustrade and veranda and cupola came to mind. I had walked into the front hall of one of Andrew Porter's characters, and I was looking into the mirror of the hall tree. But only the artifacts were there, and these, surely in their minds, in high disarray. The house itself was modest enough, especially compared to what they had been accustomed to living in before, and to the houses in the stories.

As Helen ascended the stairs, I could not help but notice, again, her youthful, fetching carriage, her unmatronly figure, her rather shapely legs. Surely she had been the real-life model for some of the wives of Andrew's male protagonists. I glanced into the looking glass and felt like a little boy again, faced with a stern teacher who has had him wait in the hall while she goes in to the principal.

I turned and looked around at the boxes and crates in the living room, at the various articles of furniture called sideboard and chiffonier and bureau and china closet in the stories. Even their boxes were orderly! It was nothing like when we have moved and everything gets in a jumble. Then when I saw various labeling on the boxes, I realized that they had had a professional mover do the job for them. And from only blocks away! (Had I been around, I thought, I could have done the job myself for only the price of a rental truck, some packing blankets, and a man to help.) I guess they must have stored a good deal of their really big pieces, or else had them shipped to one of their other houses in other states. They must simply have had the same mover bring over what they were going to make do with for Andrew's coming fall semester at the university.

It was then that I recalled when first I had seen the man I was now waiting to see again. It was my second year at the university when those of us wanting to sign up for the graduate writing seminar that fall had heard that John Jordette was leaving and would be replaced as writer-in-residence. Jordette resigned in protest over the release of some of the university's better teachers, because they had not published enough. I don't think that you had met Jordette by then. But now that you have, I think you will agree that it would have been better for me if he had stayed. Jordette is more my kind of man; at least some of his work is more like my own. None of us writing students had really heard of Andrew Porter at the time, though it was our own ignorance, and loss, for I learned during the following year, as I read everything of his I could find, that while he was not a popular writer, he was certainly a fine one, a sort of "writer's writer" (I have mentioned this)—like, say, Chekhov.

When he walked into the classroom for the first time—and this is what I want to try to get across and to feel again—when he appeared in the doorway in a gabardine jacket (it was still plenty warm in Arundeltown) and hound's-tooth trousers and, of course, a sober necktie, I looked down at his shoes. (You know that old compulsion of mine.) He wore pigskin loafers with straps that buckled across on the outsides, and I knew without ever having seen such shoes before that they were English. In fact, something about him seemed essentially English. He'd a patrician face—delicately longish nose, pointed chin, alternately smallish and widish mouth that somehow went to the side at certain times, and eyes...his eyes were playfully light. His sandy hair was beginning to thin, but still he seemed in his prime. I felt that a British actor had come to teach us how writing was done.

Until he spoke. Then the soft, Southern resonance of his voice put me—and, I assumed, the rest of the eager bunch of us—at our ease. And there was quite a diverse group in that class: a Harvard Ph.D. in theology writing a novel about a two Harvard Ph.D.s writing dissertations (one about Doctor Johnson, and a good part of it included); a beatnik type who wrote random, effortless stories about hippies; a young woman who sought in everything I saw of hers to re-capture the essence of eighteenth-century London and Tom Jones village; and several shades of aspiring writers between the extremes—all in twelve students. Mister Porter's voice cut across all the backgrounds. When he read to us, there was only the story he'd chosen (though never one of his own).

I studied him that first day, as if I were a painter and he my model. He reminded me of someone I had known as well as myself. And when, several weeks into the course, he began calling me Gabe, while retaining "Mister" and "Miss" and the Southern "Miz" So-and-So for the others, I felt certain that already he'd singled me out for special favor. It could have been that, like so many others, he simply tired of my vowel-laden surname, though I didn't think so back then. Besides, I—among them all, I assumed—had written him for permission to enroll before he arrived at the university, and I had received a post card, one which I still have tucked away somewhere, in reply. I can quote it verbatim: "If Mr. Jordette recommends that you be admitted to English 501, 502, then you may consider that you have my permission. Would you ask him to write a line of recommendation and take it, along with this card, to whoever is registering people for the course? Of if Mr. Jordette is not in town, simply present the card. Sincerely yours, Andrew Porter." Later, when I became a teacher, I had occasion to write a similar card to a student. Actually, I used some of the exact wording. (I don't have to tell you who the student was; you know how badly things turned out after his betrayal.) I have no idea what the others in that seminar did concerning permission to enroll.

Well, that is some of what went through my mind as I waited for Andrew's message. I tried to look out the window to see you, but already there were lace curtains on the windows and Oriental rugs on the floor, and I would have had to negotiate a fairly circuitous route to get to the window and then draw the curtain, and I had the feeling that Helen would by then return and find me in a compromising situation—as if I were snooping, that is. So I remained in the darkened vestibule, there being only a high windowpane in the oaken door's beautiful paneling, and no side windows.

She must have descended on cat's feet, for by the time I felt Helen's presence on the stairs above me she was already halfway down and I was looking once again at her attractiveness and thinking that I should not be, not so openly anyway. So I turned my head and said something that must have come out as, "Well, how is he?" I remember saying whatever it was exactly that I said very kindly, softly, as if I were there to visit a hospital patient.

"I am afraid that the move has been too much for him. He is resting." She said this very calmly, with only a bare trace of consideration for the visitor standing before her, or so the visitor thought. Was this the same woman who had once entertained me in her sitting room, who had provided a meal for a dozen or so students and their spouses and dates? Perhaps she'd even cooked it herself. Was this Helen Smythe Porter, whose paintings I had viewed in galleries, who had once suggested a trip abroad for the four of us? If it was, I thought, some perverse Dorian-Gray syndrome might have possessed her. Either that, or she had ice water in her veins. Perhaps that is the origin of the term "blue blood" (ha-ha).

But of course! She, too, had read the review! They had discussed it openly and had arrived at the conclusion that I, a former student and one-time friend, had dared to criticize my master. I was, in her eyes as I stood before her, a turncoat! There could be no other answer. For I had once been welcome in her home, and now I had become the enemy, an intruder. I could not wait to get out to light and air. If this was the price of greatness, I thought, better to live a quiet life in the little magazines.

"So he's feeling poorly?" I said, still kindly. I was thinking of you, if you will believe it. I was thinking of the children, of little Falstaff. But mainly, I must admit, I was concerned with what I was certain would be a deflation of spirit in me so complete that I might not ever again feel the same about Andrew.

"Yes, he is. He's not been well, you know, since his illness."

The "you know" seemed freighted with meaning: that I should know, but did not. I then remembered having heard from a friend that Andrew had had a small bout of sickness of some kind, but that he had recovered completely. Andrew himself had said nothing on the telephone the day before about feeling ill. (It must have been something to do with *noblesse oblige*.) Still, I had the distinct impression that she was protecting him from me. "Oh, I'm sorry," I must have said. I was thinking that these were people accustomed, in another time at least, to having servants, and in spite of my resentment for the privileged, in the particular frame of mind I found myself in, I was saying cordial things, giving them their due. I suppose that I could have spoken out, but I realized that I was, after all, in the presence of, in the very house of, the real thing, and I shied at the prospect.

"And how is your painting going?" I asked her.

She seemed not to want to talk about it, seemed almost surprised that I should even know about it and should be so bold as to bring it up so familiarly if I did. Nonetheless, I think that she must have smiled as she said, "Very well, thank you." But not a word about my writing. And I had sent Andrew a copy of my last story. (Do you suppose that they do not, after all, talk about such things to one another? That perhaps the Porters did not even discuss the review after all? That maybe Andrew never even showed it to her?)

I could feel her urging me to the door, though she was perfectly composed and made no actual move. She didn't need to; her presence was commanding! Then suddenly she spoke. "Could I get you something to drink, some lemonade, perhaps? There may be something in the refrigerator—."

"Oh, no. No, thank you. I have to be getting on. My family is outside, waiting," I said, or something similar.

"Well, I would like to have them in, but—." She glanced around at the boxes, at what she probably considered to be chaos.

"Oh, that's all right," I said. "I understand. We certainly know how moving is."

And then we were in the yard.

Why you did not get out of the car is a puzzle to me. Certainly you respected—and still do, I take it—Helen's work as a painter. Yet while she spoke to the children, you just sat there without so much as scolding them for playing in the flowers. I had to do that. All the time I was thinking that we might still salvage something of the visit if only the two of *you* might connect. I suppose that, by then, I had accepted Andrew's illness (or whatever it was, though if our positions had been reversed, I would have had him up to my room if I had been drawing my last breaths).

Helen remarked after the "adorable" children, then walked calmly to the car and you. I lingered in the yard, ostensibly to look after Andy and Marie, but I used the occasion to inspect the upper windows and I wondered which one of them looked out from Andrew's sick room. I thought that I heard music up there—Bach or Mozart, surely—and already the title for a story came to me. If ever I wrote it, I decided in that moment, I would call it "Distant Music." (The title and the feeling that came with it were familiar; I had the notion that it had already been done.) And I thought, too, as I looked up, that I knew now what was meant by the house of fiction, with its windows as portals of the imagination. If Andrew were looking out—and I could not tell if he were or not because of the glare—surely he was looking kindly upon the scene and wishing that he were well. I may have the metaphor a bit confused, but you will get the idea of it.

I had the feeling that, at any moment, Andy would blurt out something like, Well, where is the man you brought us here to see? I was afraid that he might tell Helen that he was named for Andrew. Obviously she did not know, had not asked the children's names—an omission I was, ironically, thankful for. So I bent to Andy, and I told him that Mister Porter was very sick and that we would not be visiting with him today. But he had found a toad and was busy scaring Marie with it.

By then the two of you were talking softly, and when I looked over Helen was smiling genuinely, and you were—or seemed to be—as affable as if the entire situation were perfectly correct. In fact, everyone seemed in control, everyone except me, of course. Why, I wondered, could Andrew not call up his strength and make an appearance before it was too late? Or simply gesture from his window? All he had to do was speak, or rap, or—. Then it came to me that he must not have known who was there to see him. Helen had not called me by name, and I reasoned that with all of the students and former students in Andrew's life she was perhaps not to be blamed for forgetting one. But that would have meant that she must simply have told him that "some former student" was there to see him and that he was up there now ignorant of the fact that it was I. I wanted to throw a pebble at the window. I wanted to ask Helen if he had asked who had come calling on him, though he should have known. (I would have.)

But of course, I did—nor said—no such thing. Instead, I took the children to the car and occupied myself with getting them settled into the back seat while you and Helen were making small talk. Why didn't you talk of painting with her? It was such an opportunity for you! I do know that no one was using any *names*! So I stood by the car's door, looking on with what must have been an insufferable smile, and we exchanged amenities with her and had to hear her say such as, "Do come back again when you're by," when we lived half a country away and had just done that very thing, and had been rebuked. Yes, rebuked! I'm sorry, but I don't see it the way you surely must.

Still, I looked up to the windows once more. I could not help myself. I thought for a moment that I might have seen a movement, but then the light was intense up there; the trees were swaying in the brief, merciful breeze; and a bird flew by at just that moment. In spite of myself, I followed the bird. Besides, I could not actually imagine Andrew Porter looking out a window like that. But if by some chance he had been, surely he would have recognized me and righted the mistake. For, yes, I think that it must all have been some kind of error—one that began with Helen's failure to know me, was complicated by the day's events and Andrew's fatigue, and was aggravated by the possibility that, in their minds, I had betrayed him in the review.

Whatever the case—perhaps I will never know—we drove away from there. You know the rest. I remember that we were not five minutes on the road when you turned to me and said flatly: "If you ever put me, and yourself, through that again, I won't stand for it."

You knew all along what would happen. You knew that all of my orchestrations would come to nothing, that I cared more for Andrew than he did for me. You were simply letting me find it out for myself. And to give you your due, you were right—at least partially so. I suppose that the moment was awkward for you, and I think that I see what you meant by what you said, including the phrase "and yourself." But I was already mortified enough; the last thing I needed was a scolding. I am not a little boy, you know. And I meant well enough, heaven knows. I wanted to make our visit back home complete...etc.

Now that the episode is over and it stands in your mind as a—what did you call it?—as a typical example of my excesses, I have re-considered it from all angles.

❧ ❧ ❧

First, I have written of this particular incident because I recall your having said several times during the years following it that it was the real beginning of our problems. It was then, you said, that you realized for the first time that what you called—and you called it many names: hero worship, literary sickness, vanity—that what you called "only one of my problems" had smitten me even to the detriment of my family's welfare. You said that such "odd" excursions into the past and with such men were beginning to be more and more frequent, and you cited other times that I had to go to airports and make arrangements for visiting writers. You said that you were tired of my putting my family second. (Quite frankly, that is why I did not ask Stanley Arbuthnot or even Rocko Janise to stay with us when I had them read last year.)

I could have chosen another situation just as well, and perhaps I shall in future letters, but that day in Arundeltown seems, above all others, to crystallize what I am trying my best to come to terms with. If such events can be symptomatic of a kind of literary malady, however, what hope can there ever really be for us? I thought that you shared my enthusiasm, that you wanted me to be a writer, and that you yourself enjoyed some of the excitement of having such men as Andrew Porter as friends. Surely you must realize, though perhaps in a different way, that all English teachers are hero-worshippers. Then so much more dedicated a disciple is a writer!

But now that I have written about this, I have a confession to make: It is not true; that is, it is not all factual. I have invented some of it. Let me explain so that you may better see my purpose.

I have read, someplace, that a story based upon a recollection of a past time should not offend anyone because before a story-teller can write any real human being into that story he must change that person's name, surely, but he must do infinitely more than that: He must distort that person's very nature so radically that the real thing is no longer recognizable. (I paraphrase.) Andrew himself was always running into people who thought that they were models for his characters, and I am certain that he did use real people in his work. A writer often does. And even Helen in her painting. From what I have seen of your own painting, your images are only vaguely taken from what is actual. But then it is different in painting. Do you see what I am trying to get at?

Andrew very likely was inviolably ill upstairs. The only wrong Helen committed was in failing to recognize me, to recall my name. You were right to be put off by my detour—yes, it was a detour. I admit it. You do not have to tell me that the entire business of stopping by was a half-truth. Perhaps you would go so far as to call it a lie. Okay. I told Andrew when I called him that we would be driving through when, in fact, it was fifty or so miles out of our way to Washington on our next stop. But the scenery was better that way, you'll have to admit. We were, after all, on vacation, and we were supposed to be friends of the Porters.

I have altered something else I need to confess to. Andrew did say, "By all means, do stop by," but he added one small word—then— and it changed everything. "By all means, do stop by...then." How much more different it sounds, as if he were saying, *Well, in that case....* But he did say that business about their "encroaching dotage." What I left out there was that he added that it might not be a good time to stop by. That is what he said at first, that is. He did not mean that literally, I was certain. What I took that to suggest was that he did not want us to feel obliged to stop—he certainly understood that we would be "driving through," for I told him that, stretching the point, of course—what with the house they were moving into unsuitable to receive us. (You know how the Porters and others like them stand on ceremony about that sort of thing.) So I told him then that, oh, we might be taking another route, and then added hurriedly that we could just leave it open. That way, I figured, he would not have to make a definite commitment one way or another. And that way, of course, I knew that I could get at least his partial assent. So since I said the doubtful part much more emphatically, he had to agree to a doubt, and of course I knew all along that we would stop.

In the end, though, it all came out wrong. The children's and your welfare should have come first. I suppose that I was still living in my student days, searching for symbols in a living story. Why, Andy didn't find a toad in the garden. It wasn't even a frog. Hell, it wasn't even a garden! What he found was a common worm, by the side of the house where a few flowers grew. It was not Bach or Mozart I thought I heard. No, that was not it at all, not at all. That was pure invention. There was no music whatsoever that day. What I heard when Helen opened the upstairs door, not when I was gazing at the window from outside, was the sound of a television program in progress…and I refused the image of the man above convalescing in such a common way.

It has been no simple matter for me to resolve the events of that day. In fact, I did not know very much of this before I began to write to you, and only discovered the full truth of it as I wrote the preceding paragraph. Perhaps now I have the real beginning of my story to be titled—it has a famous origin—"Distant Music." Now I may be able to write it in the way it must be written. I hope that you will better understand and that we can put that part of the past behind us, for good….

▸ ▸ ▸

Your letter arrived a week ago, at this point in my own.

Your words make what I have written sound foolish and vain. Nevertheless, I have decided to send all of this anyway, so that you will better know my perceptions or, I should say, misperceptions. Your letter is humbling; I want to go to my knees before you. For I think that you must be prescient in a way I can never hope to be. I have never been so severely stopped. It has taken me this week to be able to assimilate your comments and to be able to go on.

You are quite right to chastise me for my other letters to you by telling me that I wrote them as if I were writing the first drafts of stories, not letters to my wife. I suppose that is why it took several of them to get an answer from you. (Am I right?) I apologize for having you think that I would use our private life, as you put it, as a springboard to my stories. Most of all do I regret your saying that when you see what the striving for the creation of art does to some people, you don't care if you never paint again. Still, you are, at least potentially, so much a better artist than I am a writer. And your observation that life comes first, I cannot argue with: "Without life, there can be no art, so it's a dead-end for you [me] or anyone else who seeks immortality without mortality." How beautifully perceptive, how succinctly put.

I had the hubris to dare to—how did I put it?—attempt to describe the scene before our first house from your angle of vision. Had I only known! When we were there on Sycamore Street—and how coincidental that you should recall in the letter that very incident, and how wrong I was about it!—when we stopped there, I felt, or thought I felt, or invented what I have described earlier—. But you say that you were thinking of the two years you had lived there with me and that you still had not adjusted to red dirt. Red dirt! It ought to be black, you say; dirt is black. Clay is red! Frankly, I, too, had trouble with the clay. Arno has some, but the mountains all around it are of rich, black humus. You were thinking as you looked out the side window, you say, that the heat and humidity had left you drained of energy so much of the time, and you were recalling how much you hated the rigid class system there, how you had to fight that ignorant principal as she openly showed prejudice against your black students, and how, in the face of it all, you were called a "bleeding heart" by such as that law student from Richmond, married to (what was her name?), who taught with you. Yes, I now know how much you went through: teaching seven hours straight without so much as a restroom break, fighting the anger of difficult white parents who didn't want their children associating with your black students, trying to keep order in the classroom and to teach something to those deprived and barely intelligible young black kids, then grading papers and planning lessons all evening. I hope you remember that I visited your class a few times and taught—or tried to teach—a lesson or two in grammar. I was mighty proud of you when you took your class to that snobbish country club when the invitation was given with the tacit understanding that no teacher would dare take a "nigra." You integrated that swimming pool single-handedly!

Remember the Good Neighbor Pledge? Somebody at the university circulated a petition affirming that any family—meaning, of course, any black family—could live any place in Arundeltown (as if they—or we, for that matter—could ever afford to!). We signed along with several hundred others, and all our names were printed below the pledge, in bold print, in the newspaper. When I had my conference with Andrew the day after it came out and we talked about it, I suggested that a man in his position could do so much more good by signing his name. Well, I proffered the petition, and he signed it. Then an addendum was published, and his name appeared, all by itself, under the *P*'s. (I wonder if he ever regretted it.)

Oh, yes, I realize now that it wasn't easy for you, though at the time I thought that I was, well, pulling my own by reading, studying every spare minute (you know how slowly I read) and writing papers, competing for *A*'s and teaching night classes for Continuing Education. How did you put it?: "...enjoying your [my] calm campus and having a beer at the graduate club and studying stimulating writers." It is true that it was enjoyable, but I must confess to you that, throughout it all, I was scared stiff! I was up against some of the best minds in the country—teachers and students. I was the only one in graduate English with a bachelor's degree in engineering, a veteran on the G.I. Bill. I wasn't just reading brilliant works of modern (arcane) poetry and fiction but absurdist drama, existential stuff I didn't care for, Jacobean drama, and fat eighteenth-century novels I thought I'd never get through. And Shakespeare! Mister Harrington was apparently one of the scholars on the Bard; we had virtually to commit to memory a play a week. (Closed-book exam: In act II, scene III of *As You Like It*, discuss...). On top of it all, and above all (though on stolen time), I was writing my own stories for Andrew's class. (Frankly, after my military experiences, I was swimming in a sea of literary luxury and loving it.)

But now I see myself back there for what I must have appeared to be to you. Why I didn't know at the time, at parties for instance, that I became "loud, drunk, egotistical, and flirtatious," I cannot say. Perhaps I was too stimulated. And, no, I was not sharing protesting views on the war, or engaging in the pros and cons of our turbulent times. I was not speaking out with compassion about people on the bottom rung of the economic ladder. (Could it have been that, subconsciously, I was escaping from what I had known of some of this myself?) I suppose that I must have been trying to impress. And I must not have been so helpful at home. Yes, I must have put myself first; I must have idolized the writers I read, and those I met.

But now that I am able, with the help of your sobering letter, to think tranquilly about it, I am reminded of a couple of lines of poetry. Imagine yourself the speaker: "What is it in you that I love so much/And like so little?" (I may have the "like" and "love" reversed, and I can't for the life of me remember the poet.) Please, let it not be that you might already have reached something of the same impasse.

I do recall, now, mentioning our visit to the Porters' in an earlier letter, probably as a prelude to this one. I suppose that is why you chose to write about it. When you say that you understand that I cared for Andrew as a teacher and as a friend but that I put too much faith in his friendship, you are, evidently, right. And, yes, I do now understand that he must have hundreds of former students who have wanted to visit him or send him their stories. I thought I was special. (I am not.)

That I am "so literal-minded about some things and so symbolic about others" is something I cannot help, though. I would like to change, and perhaps I will be able to someday if I can quit fooling myself that I can ever really be a writer, or that I can ever write about anything that people will care to read. Maybe, with help, I will be able to give it up altogether, but what's to be done when you are driven but without the talent or—irony of ironies!—even the proper raw material?

There again, you are probably right when you say that seeing into a woman's mind is not one of my strengths and that I should stick to what I do best— though you do not actually say what I do best—and forget the embellishment. (It's what a number of rejecting editors have told me.) Maybe Andrew, too, was trying to tell me that I should write about what I know and forget being literary. But I am, honestly, surprised that you should think that I write—or try to write—like Andrew. I? Imitate Andrew Porter? As if I ever could.

Concerning that line of criticism: If you think that a sentence about a story could mean so much to him or to me and that our egos are too fragile, you are, once again, probably right. You will no doubt be thinking, once you get this, that I have made entirely too much of it all: the review, the visit—all of it. Why do I make so much of things? Why, for instance, should I expect my relatives, who, except for my mother, are not natural readers, to offer comments on an occasional story I might send them, especially when they are included in so much of what I write? Why must I try to guess and second-guess whatever on earth the Porters might or might not think or do? All that business about whether or not we were going to be invited for lunch, etc., etc. It's silly, I know. Why didn't I simply talk to you about the situation? Why have a motive at all? You have told me any number of times that people don't always have to have motives; they just do things, say things. You say that we do not live in stories. Am I living inside my head, trying to write stories so much that I am forgetting the simple actions that need no motivation or conflict? You get me where it counts when you say that, frankly, you think that I may just be dreaming up a whole new story about the Porters and our visit there. What will you think now, when you read my detailed account of it? And why must I feel compelled to try to tell it, lies and all, and then to send it to you? (If I write it as a story someday, will I send it to Andrew?)

But I must be able to retain some semblance of my own integrity. When your letter came, please remember, I was on the verge of confessing my own short-sightedness.

❧ ❧ ❧

And now I make a resolution:

No longer will I consider the work of the Andrew Porters as that of living writers—men and women whom I happen to know—but as the work of writers in a great, silent anthology. In that way, perhaps I can better reconcile my own personal, familial life and duties with the agonies of the writer in me. For now I realize that one's perception of the work is altered when one knows the man. There is no such difficulty with that great host of dead writers: Their lives are over; their work alone lives.

I might have wanted at some time to imitate the style—both literary and personal—of Andrew Porter. He is still and, I suppose, always will remain my literary father. I cannot change that. But I have come to realize that there have been no balustrades or porticoes or cupolas or chiffoniers in my life (though maybe a chifforobe—ha-ha). Porte-cochère? Can't even pronounce it. To be frank, I am not even certain just what all of these things are. That over-sized sideboard I mentioned? It was like a catafalque. And, to tell the truth, though I pretended otherwise, I never really did like those old Oriental rugs such as the Porters keep scattered about. They look like thin and faded rags to me.

Which brings me, as always it seems, back to me. Remember that double-breasted, navy-blue jacket, split in the back, I had to have charged when we were broke? Well, it was to be my "boss coat." And then the fountain-pen phase I went through for a while? One day I asked the secretary if she had any ink, and she looked at me as if I were crazy and answered jokingly: "What's that?" I finally switched back to a black ballpoint, extra fine. And my so-called "ascent of Parnassus"? Little did I know at the time that those walks would turn out to be more like the doomed repetitions of Sisyphus.

Yet, as I stood that day before the Porters' house, trying, I now know, to rationalize my disappointment before we left, I fancied that Andrew lay deathly ill in his upper chamber, that he had achieved as a writer all it is humanly possible to achieve in our age, and that somehow his mantle were being passed to me by the Muses, or maybe by that bird my eyes followed. (Imagine how the bird would have delivered it!) How utterly silly of me—or of my fancy, rather!

While I'm resolving and confessing: My little review of Porter's novella was published in a college magazine with next-to-no circulation, and he would not have heard about it, much less have *read* it, had I not sent a copy to him. Yes, I sent it to him. I thought that he might be pleased. Who knows? Maybe he was in some small way. Still, it seems to me now that I might have been revealing something of his fictional world alien to myself. Let me explain, if you'll pardon the expression.

I said earlier that Andrew reminded me of someone I knew as well as I knew myself. And I certainly did for...it *was* myself. It was an older version of the face I had seen in the looking glass every day of my life—strangely a projection of my own face into an older age. (No wonder so many people at that conference took Jordette's introduction of me as "Andrew's boy" literally.) But, of course, it was all high confusion, subconsciously brought on, I suppose, because I had adopted Andrew's mannerisms, his style (certainly not his writing), his speech and mien. I suppose, for a while there, I was his "boy," in more ways than one.

Finally, however, my "style" and his are far apart, as are our worlds, though I would like to think that in some ways I will remain blood-and-quill brother to him. My own material—the world and people of Arno—could never accommodate such refinements as his. No amount of care and subtlety can ever make an Andrew Porter character believable in the streets and houses of my hometown. For no one—certainly not the boy who walked out early one morning to commit his modest streets to memory, then went off and, for a little while, thought that he was somebody else, or somebody—for no one like that ever lived there.

So that is my conclusion. I will write when and as I can, and I plan to use other such incidents to make myself better known to you. In the meantime, thank you for allowing me the discovery, and please love the children enough for both of us until you will let me be with all of you once more.

By the way, you probably don't have to worry about ever seeing any of this in print. Magazines, I am told, are on the whole "distrustful" of stories about writers. Some taboo-become-legend started by somebody-or-other. I cannot for the life of me imagine why.

About the Author

Joseph Maiolo was born in West Virginia, was raised in the Cumberland Mountains of southwest Virginia, and has earned degrees from the University of Virginia (M.A.), the University of North Carolina at Greensboro (M.F.A.), and the United States Naval Academy (B.S.). He is presently a professor of English at the University of Minnesota Duluth, where he teaches literature and fiction writing. His short stories have been published in *The Sewanee Review*, *Ploughshares*, *Shenandoah*, *The Texas Review*, *The Greensboro Review*, other magazines, and anthologies. Several of his stories and a novella have won national awards, including citation in *The Best American Short Stories*, a Pushcart Prize, two National Endowment for the Arts Literary Fellowships, and three PEN/Syndicated Fiction Awards. Two of the PEN prize stories have been read on National Public Radio's "The Sound of Writing." Maiolo's work has also received a Bush Artist Fellowship and a Loft-McKnight Award of Distinction in Fiction. "The Girl and the Serpent," an excerpt from his memoir in progress, was published by Beacon Press (Boston) in *Resurrecting Grace: Remembering Catholic Childhoods*. Maiolo has completed two novels, assembled a collection of his short stories, and is revising an Appalachian Virginia memoir.

Maiolo has also co-written the screenplays My Turkish Missile Crisis and Mountain, both currently seeking production, and has written an original screenplay, Leif's Tune. His co-written play, *The Man Who Moved a Mountain*, has enjoyed several productions in southwest Virginia; another play, *Once on Buffalo Mountain*, was dramatically read at the Appalachian Festival of Plays and Playwrights at the Barter Theatre in Abingdon, Virginia. Maiolo has written the treatment for *Moving Mountains*, a video tribute to Robert Childress, in production at the time of this publication.

Additionally, Maiolo has written the lyrics to a suite of four songs—folk, classical, jazz, and rock—which has been performed in concert with orchestra and singers.